Yannick Grotholt – Writer

Comicon – Artist

PAPERCUTZ™

New York

LEGO® CHIMA Graphic Novels Available from PAPERCUTZ™

LEGO
LEGENDS OF CHIMA
ALL-NEW GRAPHIC NOVEL SERIES!
HIGH RISK!
PAPERCUTZ

Graphic Novel #1
"High Risk!"

LEGO
LEGENDS OF CHIMA
THE RIGHT DECISION

Graphic Novel #2
"The Right Decision"

LEGO
LEGENDS OF CHIMA
CHI QUEST!
PAPERCUTZ

Graphic Novel #3
"CHI Quest!"

FSC
www.fsc.org
MIX
Paper from responsible sources
FSC® C016245

LEGO LEGENDS OF CHIMA graphic novels are available for $7.99 in paperback, $12.99 hardcover. Available from booksellers everywhere. You can also order online from Papercutz.com. Or call 1-800-886-1223, Monday through Friday, 9-5 EST. MC, Visa, and AmEx accepted. To order by mail, please add $4.00 for postage and handling for first book ordered, $1.00 for each additional book and make check payable to NBM Publishing. Send to: Papercutz, 160 Broadway, Suite 700, East Wing, New York, NY 10038.

LEGO LEGENDS OF CHIMA graphic novels are also available digitally wherever e-books are sold.

Papercutz.com

LEGENDS OF CHIMA
#3 "CHI Quest!"

Yannick Grotholt – Writer
Comicon – Artist
(Miguel Sanchez – Pencils
Marc Alberich – Inks
Oriol San Julian – Color)
Bryan Senka – Letterer
Alexander Lu – Editorial Intern
Beth Scorzato – Production Coordinator
Michael Petranek – Editor
Jim Salicrup
Editor-in-Chief

ISBN: 978-1-62991-076-5 paperback edition
ISBN: 978-1-62991-077-2 hardcover edition

Printed in Canada
October 2014 by Friesens Printing
1 Printer Way
Altona, MB R0G 0B0

Papercutz books may be purchased for business or promotional use. For information on bulk purchases please contact Macmillan Corporate and Premium Sales Department at (800) 221-7945 x5442.

Distributed by Macmillan
First Papercutz Printing

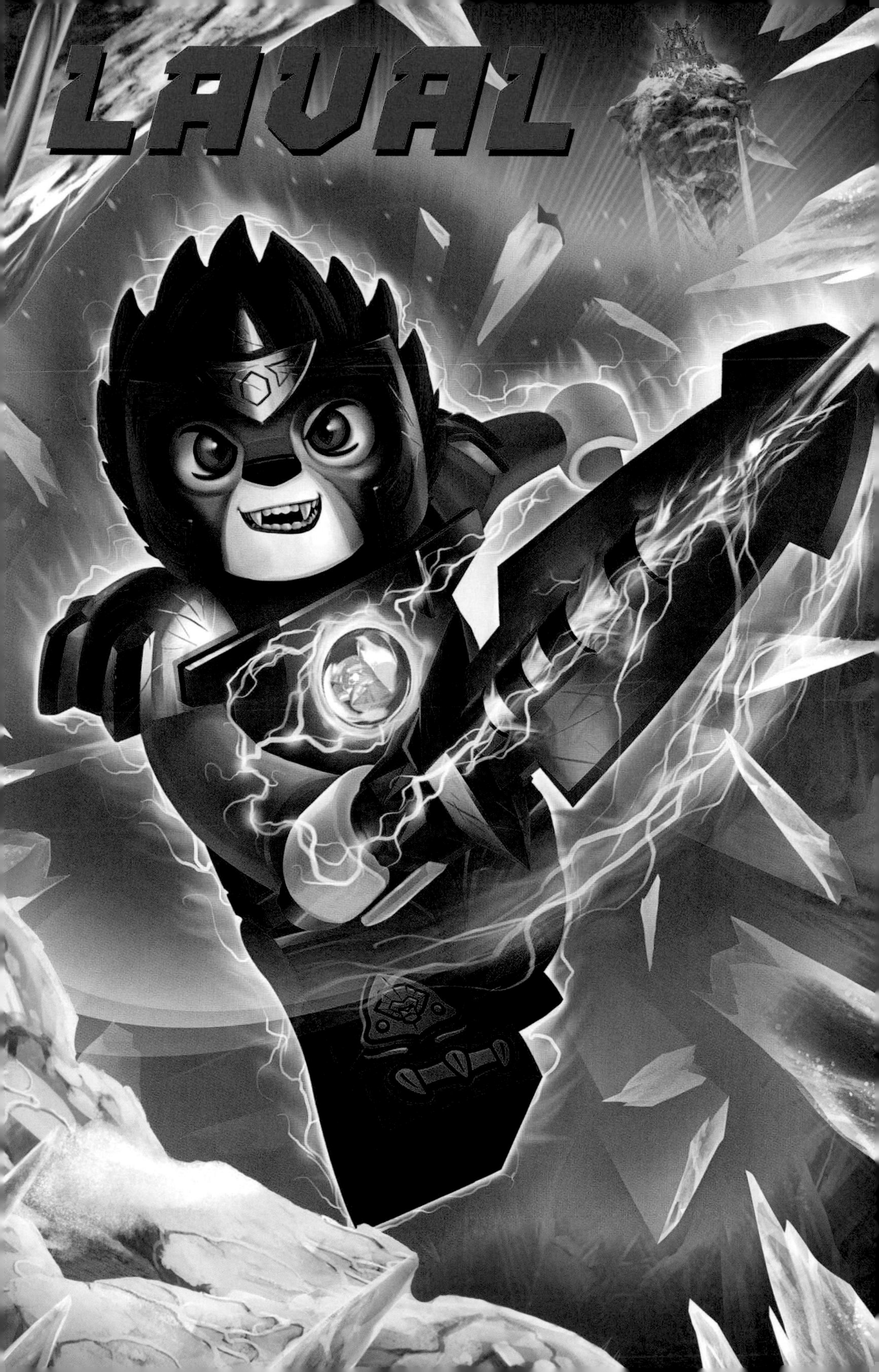
LAVAL

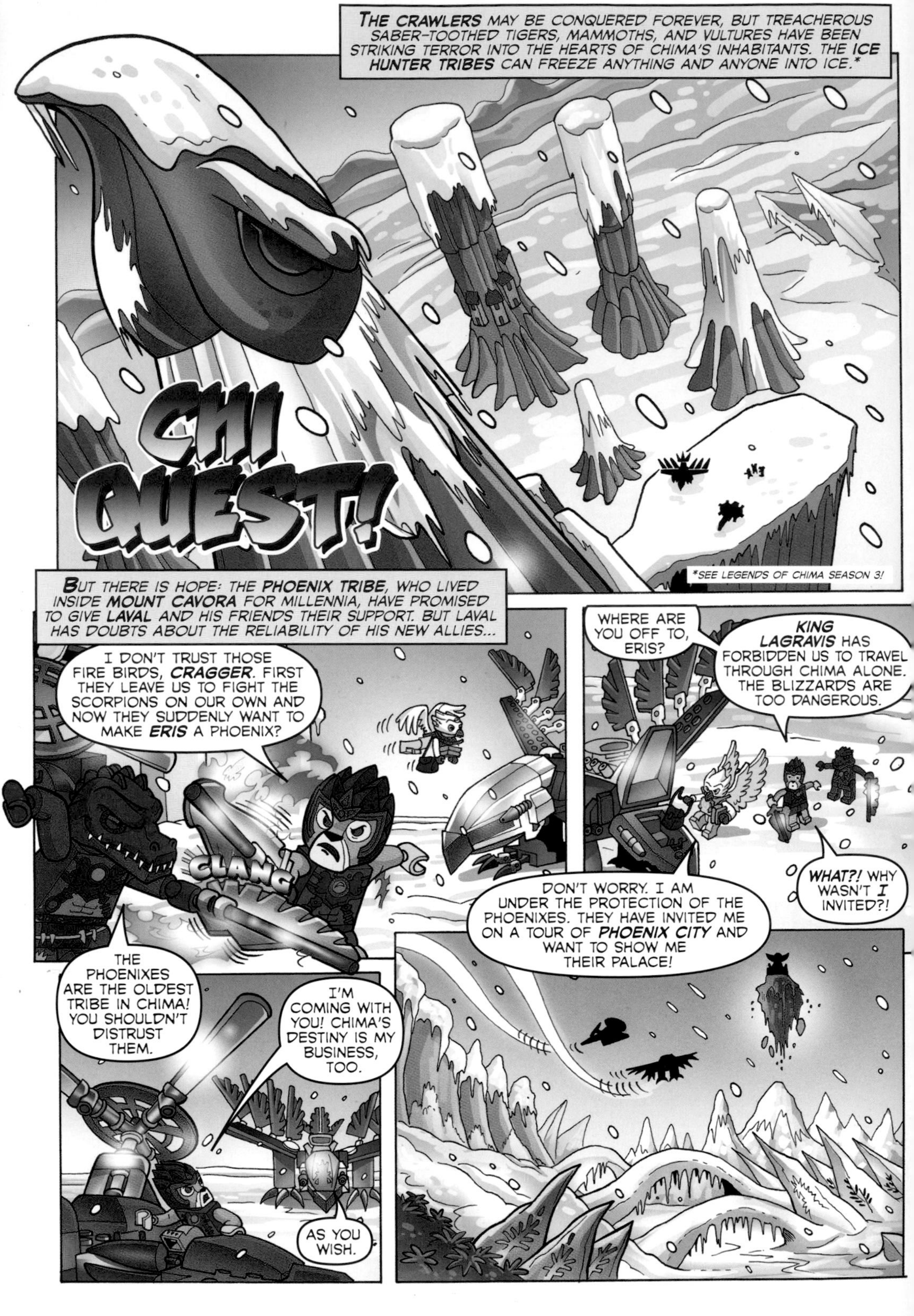
THE CRAWLERS MAY BE CONQUERED FOREVER, BUT TREACHEROUS SABER-TOOTHED TIGERS, MAMMOTHS, AND VULTURES HAVE BEEN STRIKING TERROR INTO THE HEARTS OF CHIMA'S INHABITANTS. THE ICE HUNTER TRIBES CAN FREEZE ANYTHING AND ANYONE INTO ICE.*
CHI QUEST!
*SEE LEGENDS OF CHIMA SEASON 3!
BUT THERE IS HOPE: THE PHOENIX TRIBE, WHO LIVED INSIDE MOUNT CAVORA FOR MILLENNIA, HAVE PROMISED TO GIVE LAVAL AND HIS FRIENDS THEIR SUPPORT. BUT LAVAL HAS DOUBTS ABOUT THE RELIABILITY OF HIS NEW ALLIES...
I DON'T TRUST THOSE FIRE BIRDS, CRAGGER. FIRST THEY LEAVE US TO FIGHT THE SCORPIONS ON OUR OWN AND NOW THEY SUDDENLY WANT TO MAKE ERIS A PHOENIX?
CLANG
THE PHOENIXES ARE THE OLDEST TRIBE IN CHIMA! YOU SHOULDN'T DISTRUST THEM.
WHERE ARE YOU OFF TO, ERIS?
KING LAGRAVIS HAS FORBIDDEN US TO TRAVEL THROUGH CHIMA ALONE. THE BLIZZARDS ARE TOO DANGEROUS.
DON'T WORRY. I AM UNDER THE PROTECTION OF THE PHOENIXES. THEY HAVE INVITED ME ON A TOUR OF PHOENIX CITY AND WANT TO SHOW ME THEIR PALACE!
WHAT?! WHY WASN'T I INVITED?!
I'M COMING WITH YOU! CHIMA'S DESTINY IS MY BUSINESS, TOO.
AS YOU WISH.

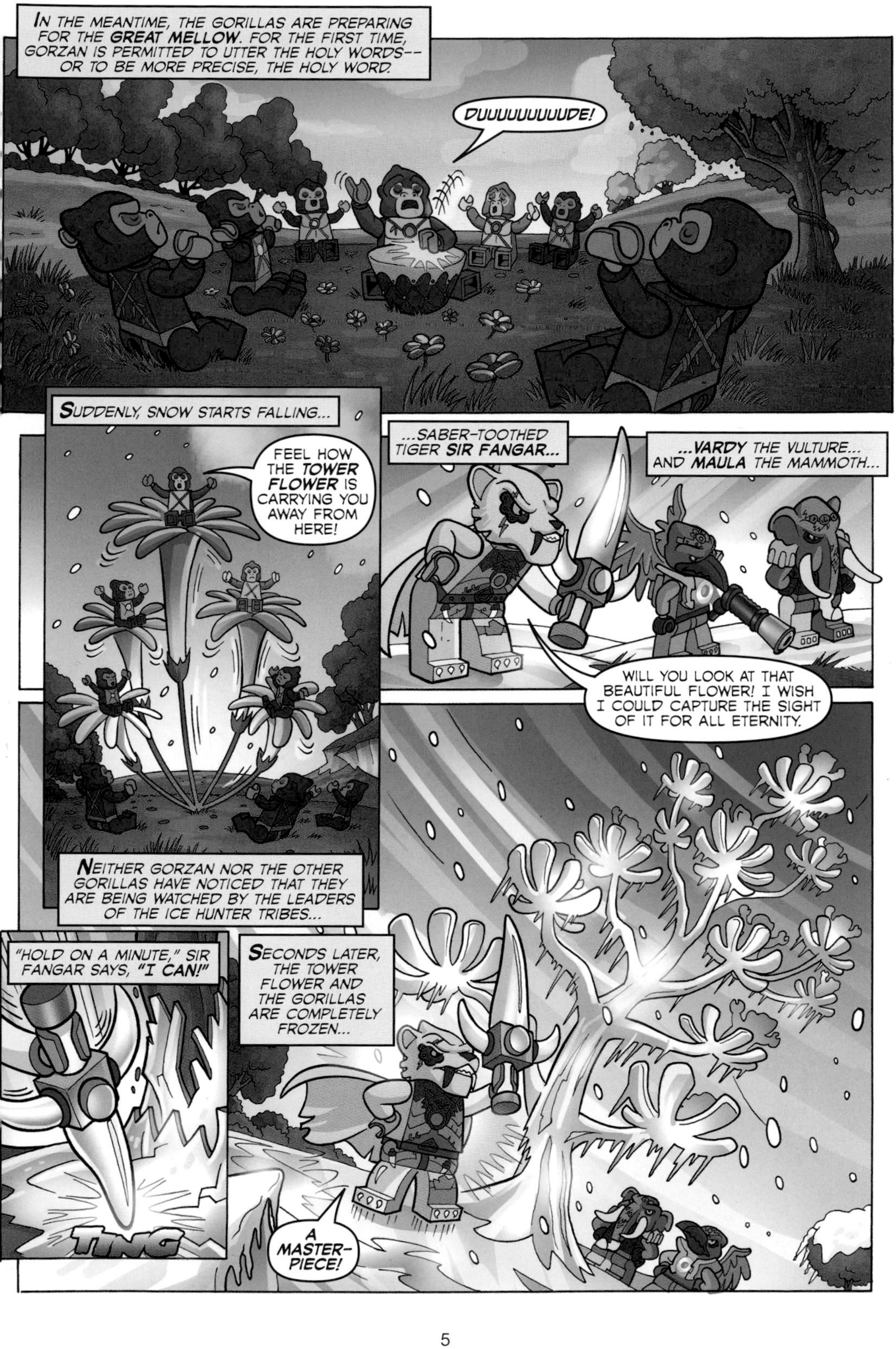
IN THE MEANTIME, THE GORILLAS ARE PREPARING FOR THE GREAT MELLOW. FOR THE FIRST TIME, GORZAN IS PERMITTED TO UTTER THE HOLY WORDS--OR TO BE MORE PRECISE, THE HOLY WORD.
DUUUUUUUUUDE!
SUDDENLY, SNOW STARTS FALLING...
FEEL HOW THE TOWER FLOWER IS CARRYING YOU AWAY FROM HERE!
...SABER-TOOTHED TIGER SIR FANGAR...
...VARDY THE VULTURE... AND MAULA THE MAMMOTH...
WILL YOU LOOK AT THAT BEAUTIFUL FLOWER! I WISH I COULD CAPTURE THE SIGHT OF IT FOR ALL ETERNITY.
NEITHER GORZAN NOR THE OTHER GORILLAS HAVE NOTICED THAT THEY ARE BEING WATCHED BY THE LEADERS OF THE ICE HUNTER TRIBES...
"HOLD ON A MINUTE," SIR FANGAR SAYS, "I CAN!"
TING
SECONDS LATER, THE TOWER FLOWER AND THE GORILLAS ARE COMPLETELY FROZEN...
A MASTER-PIECE!

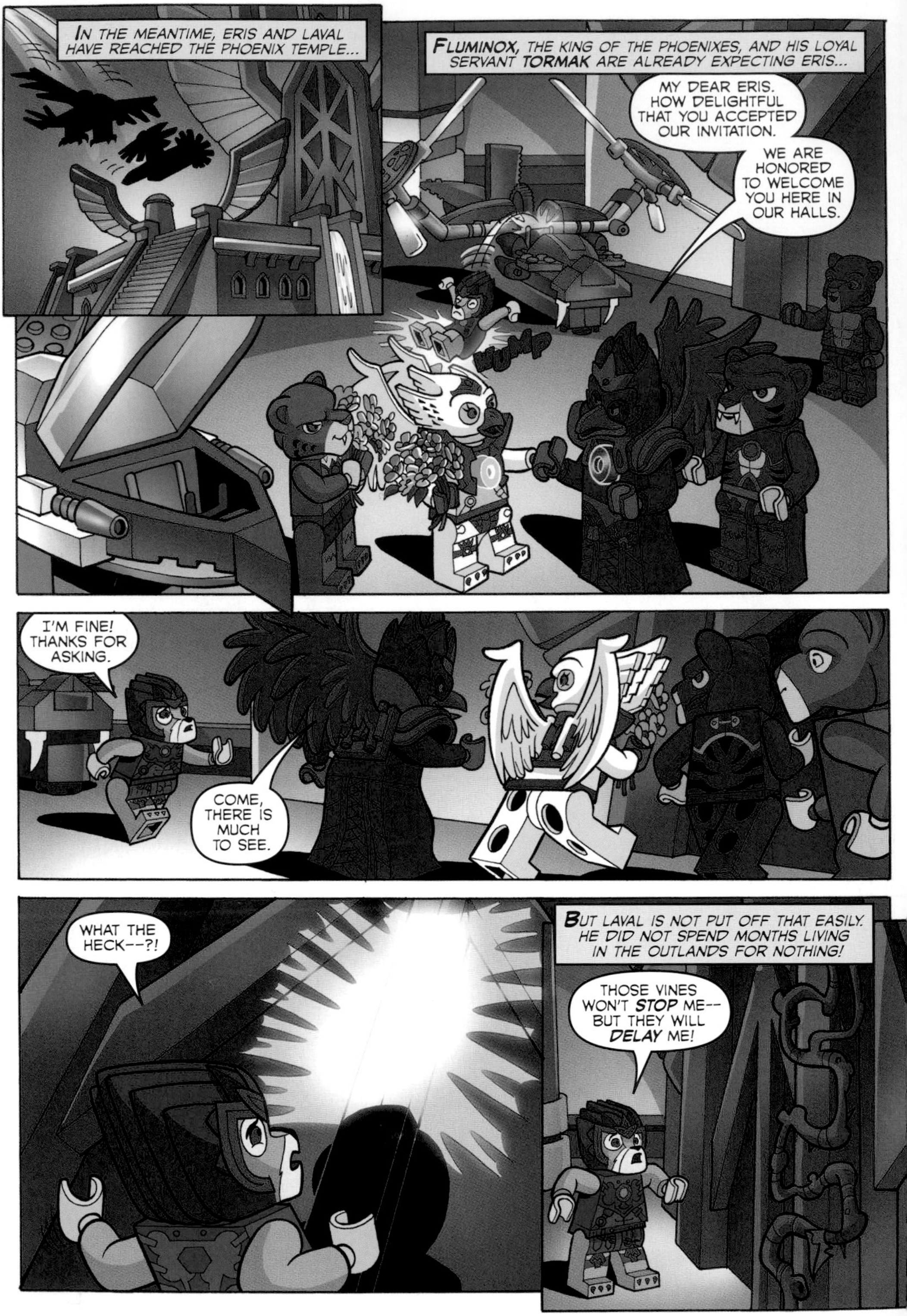
IN THE MEANTIME, ERIS AND LAVAL HAVE REACHED THE PHOENIX TEMPLE...
FLUMINOX, THE KING OF THE PHOENIXES, AND HIS LOYAL SERVANT TORMAK ARE ALREADY EXPECTING ERIS...
MY DEAR ERIS. HOW DELIGHTFUL THAT YOU ACCEPTED OUR INVITATION.
WE ARE HONORED TO WELCOME YOU HERE IN OUR HALLS.
WUMP
I'M FINE! THANKS FOR ASKING.
COME, THERE IS MUCH TO SEE.
WHAT THE HECK--?!
BUT LAVAL IS NOT PUT OFF THAT EASILY. HE DID NOT SPEND MONTHS LIVING IN THE OUTLANDS FOR NOTHING!
THOSE VINES WON'T STOP ME-- BUT THEY WILL DELAY ME!

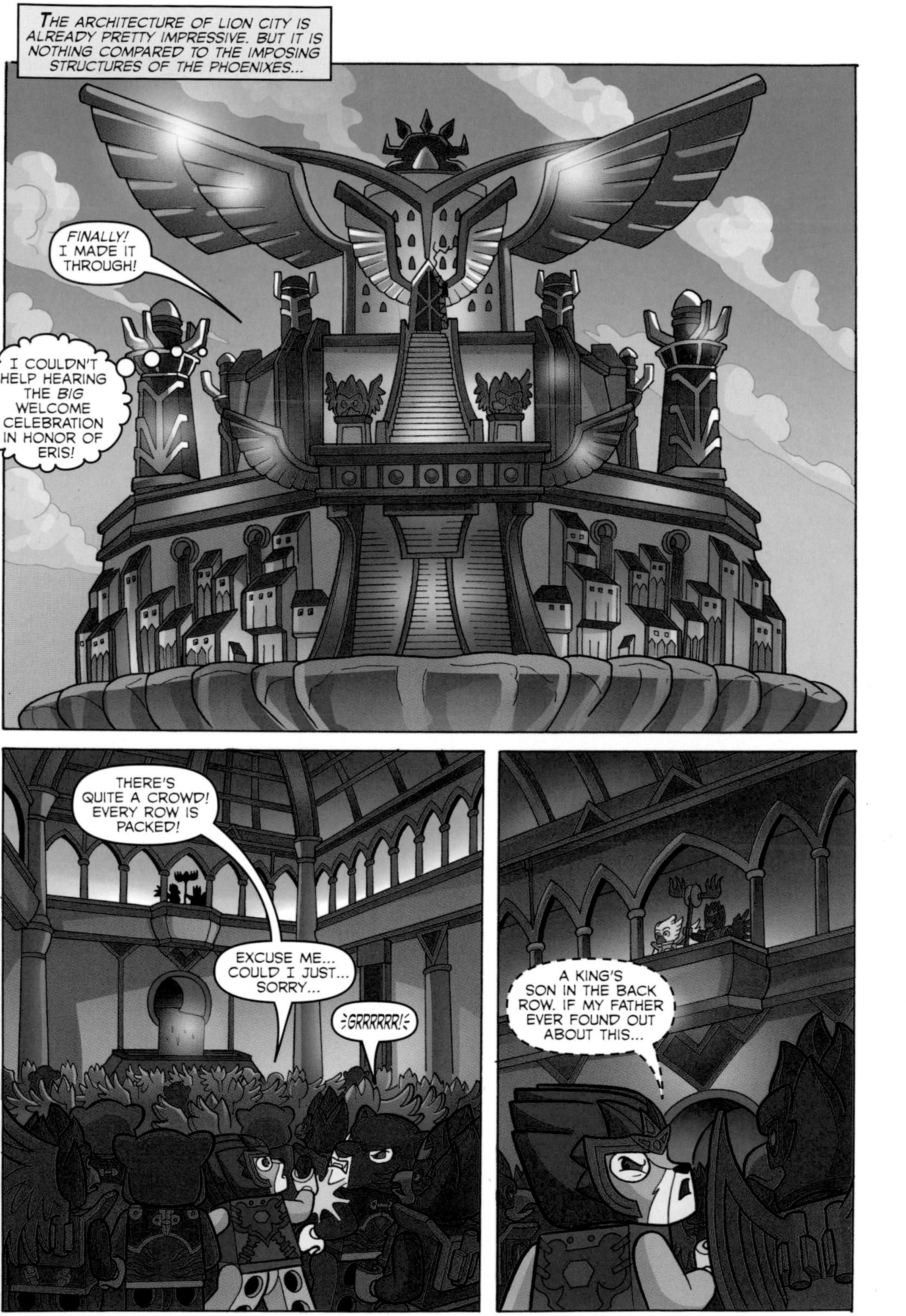
THE ARCHITECTURE OF LION CITY IS ALREADY PRETTY IMPRESSIVE. BUT IT IS NOTHING COMPARED TO THE IMPOSING STRUCTURES OF THE PHOENIXES...
FINALLY! I MADE IT THROUGH!
I COULDN'T HELP HEARING THE *BIG* WELCOME CELEBRATION IN HONOR OF ERIS!
THERE'S QUITE A CROWD! EVERY ROW IS PACKED!
EXCUSE ME... COULD I JUST... SORRY...
GRRRRRR!
A KING'S SON IN THE BACK ROW. IF MY FATHER EVER FOUND OUT ABOUT THIS...

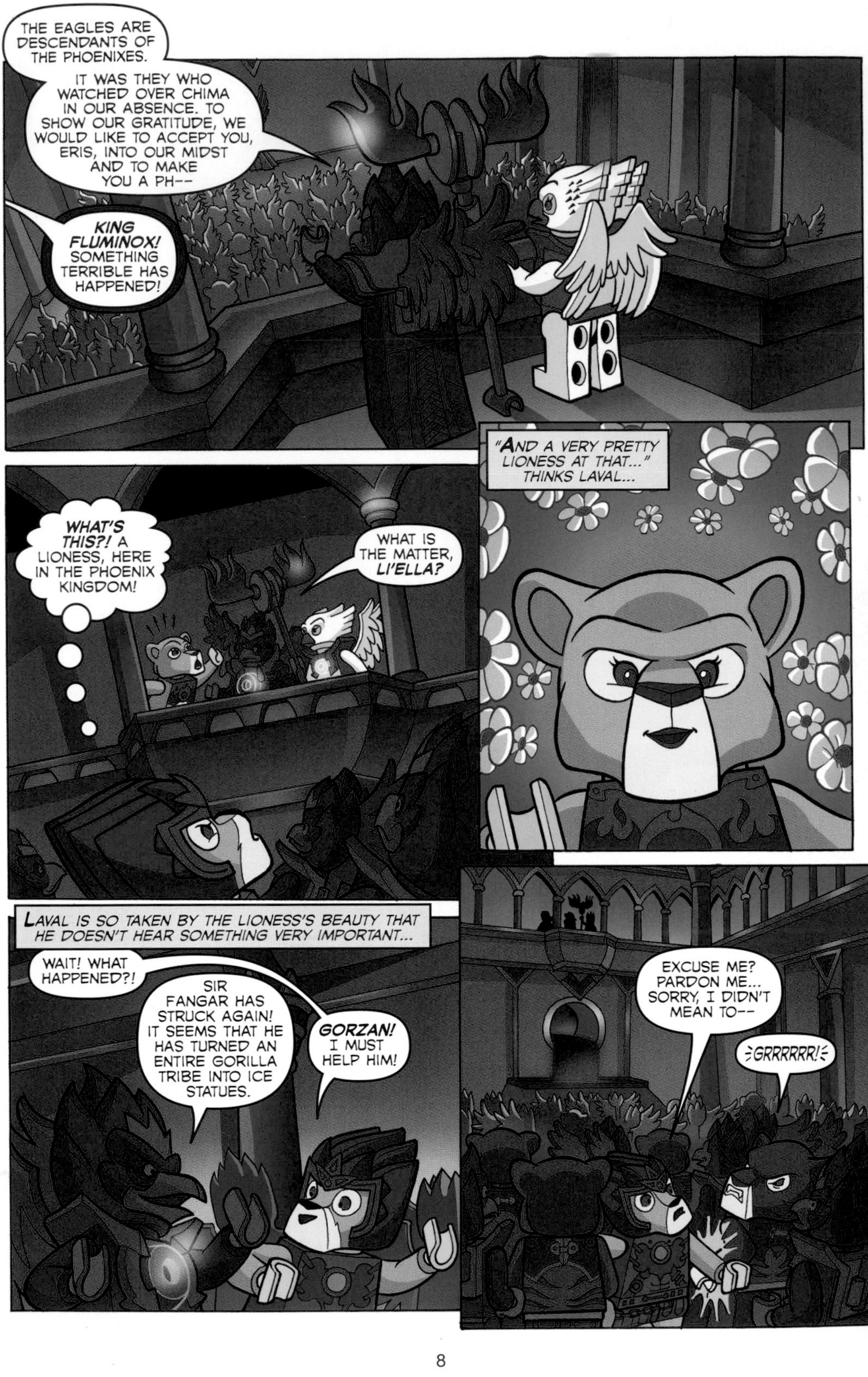
THE EAGLES ARE DESCENDANTS OF THE PHOENIXES.
IT WAS THEY WHO WATCHED OVER CHIMA IN OUR ABSENCE. TO SHOW OUR GRATITUDE, WE WOULD LIKE TO ACCEPT YOU, ERIS, INTO OUR MIDST AND TO MAKE YOU A PH--
KING FLUMINOX! SOMETHING TERRIBLE HAS HAPPENED!
WHAT'S THIS?! A LIONESS, HERE IN THE PHOENIX KINGDOM!
WHAT IS THE MATTER, LI'ELLA?
"AND A VERY PRETTY LIONESS AT THAT..." THINKS LAVAL...
LAVAL IS SO TAKEN BY THE LIONESS'S BEAUTY THAT HE DOESN'T HEAR SOMETHING VERY IMPORTANT...
WAIT! WHAT HAPPENED?!
SIR FANGAR HAS STRUCK AGAIN! IT SEEMS THAT HE HAS TURNED AN ENTIRE GORILLA TRIBE INTO ICE STATUES.
GORZAN! I MUST HELP HIM!
EXCUSE ME? PARDON ME... SORRY, I DIDN'T MEAN TO--
GRRRRRR!

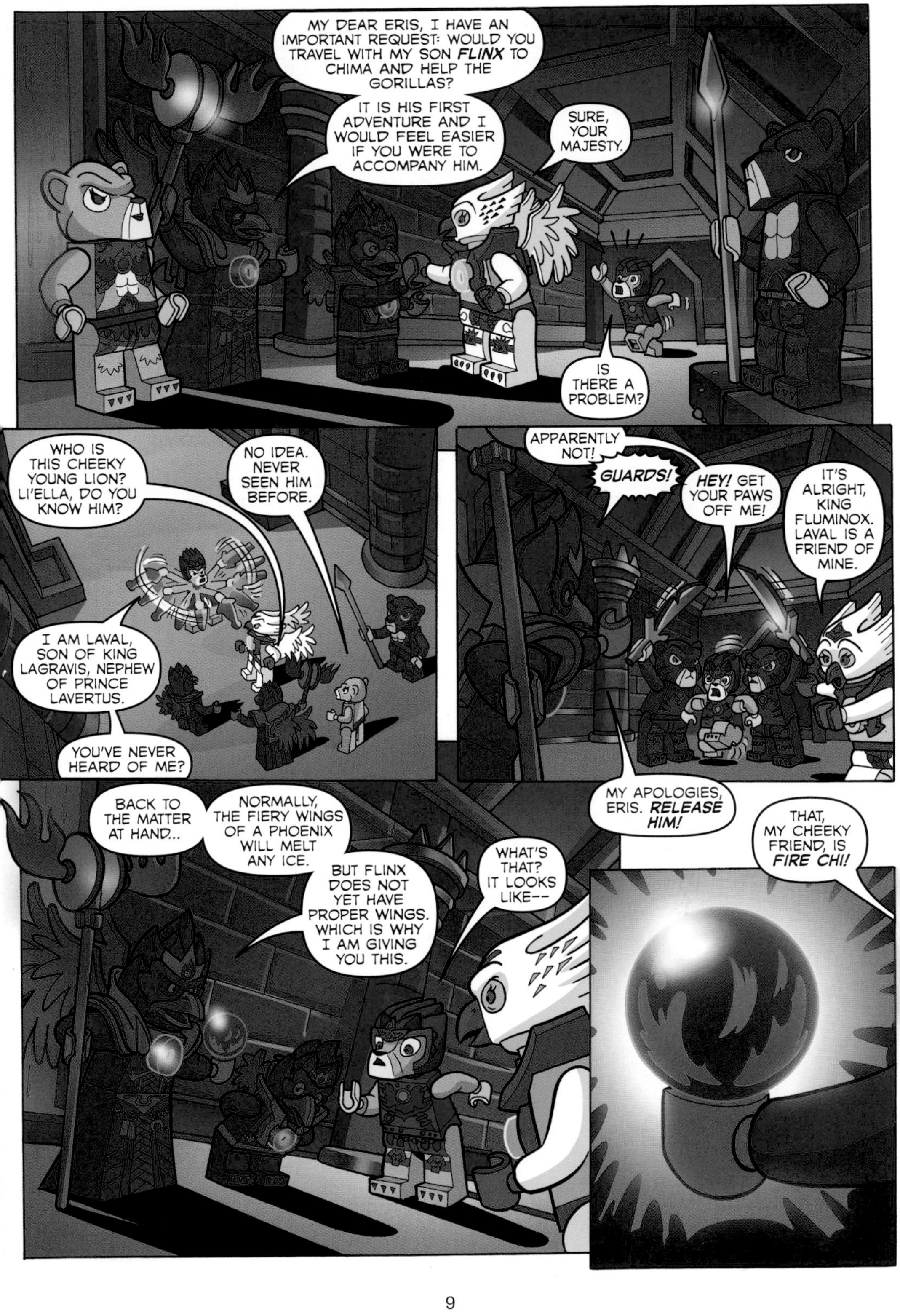

MY DEAR ERIS, I HAVE AN IMPORTANT REQUEST: WOULD YOU TRAVEL WITH MY SON *FLINX* TO CHIMA AND HELP THE GORILLAS?
IT IS HIS FIRST ADVENTURE AND I WOULD FEEL EASIER IF YOU WERE TO ACCOMPANY HIM.
SURE, YOUR MAJESTY.
IS THERE A PROBLEM?
WHO IS THIS CHEEKY YOUNG LION? LI'ELLA, DO YOU KNOW HIM?
NO IDEA. NEVER SEEN HIM BEFORE.
I AM LAVAL, SON OF KING LAGRAVIS, NEPHEW OF PRINCE LAVERTUS.
YOU'VE NEVER HEARD OF ME?
APPARENTLY NOT!
GUARDS!
HEY! GET YOUR PAWS OFF ME!
IT'S ALRIGHT, KING FLUMINOX. LAVAL IS A FRIEND OF MINE.
MY APOLOGIES, ERIS. ***RELEASE HIM!***
BACK TO THE MATTER AT HAND...
NORMALLY, THE FIERY WINGS OF A PHOENIX WILL MELT ANY ICE.
BUT FLINX DOES NOT YET HAVE PROPER WINGS. WHICH IS WHY I AM GIVING YOU THIS.
WHAT'S THAT? IT LOOKS LIKE--
THAT, MY CHEEKY FRIEND, IS ***FIRE CHI!***

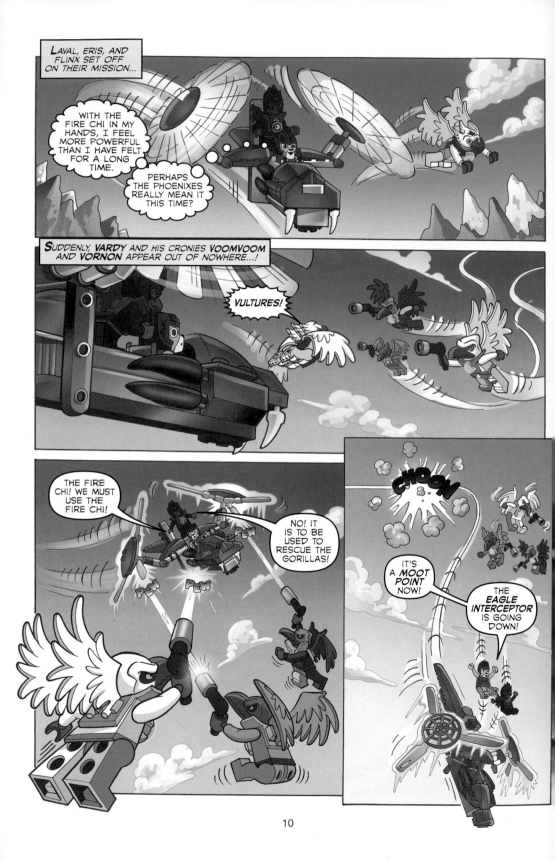

LAVAL, ERIS, AND FLINX SET OFF ON THEIR MISSION...

WITH THE FIRE CHI IN MY HANDS, I FEEL MORE POWERFUL THAN I HAVE FELT FOR A LONG TIME.

PERHAPS THE PHOENIXES REALLY MEAN IT THIS TIME?

SUDDENLY, **VARDY** AND HIS CRONIES **VOOMVOOM** AND **VORNON** APPEAR OUT OF NOWHERE...!

VULTURES!

THE FIRE CHI! WE MUST USE THE FIRE CHI!

NO! IT IS TO BE USED TO RESCUE THE GORILLAS!

PEW
PEW
PEW

CHOOM

IT'S A *MOOT POINT* NOW!

THE *EAGLE INTERCEPTOR* IS GOING DOWN!

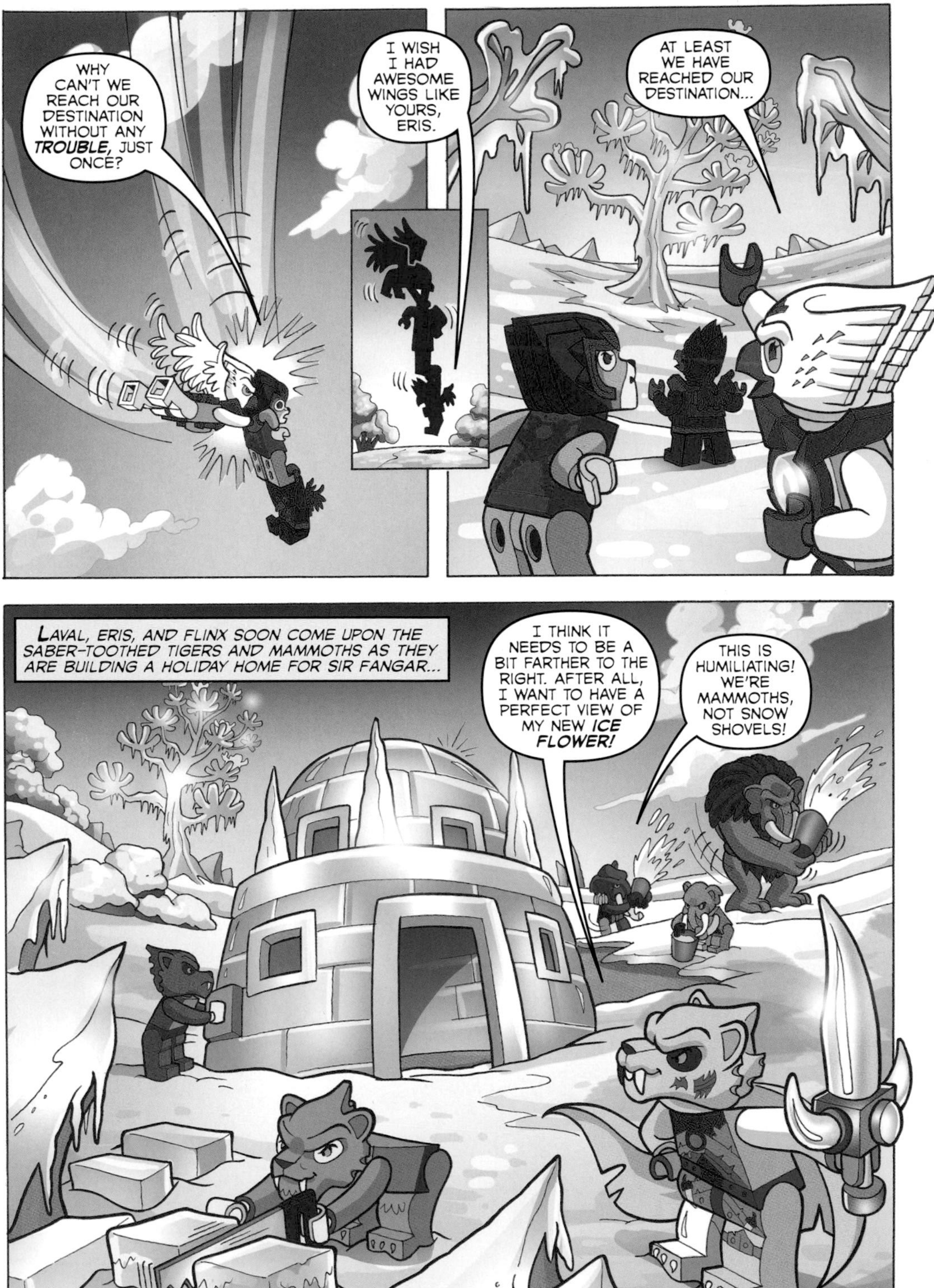
WHY CAN'T WE REACH OUR DESTINATION WITHOUT ANY TROUBLE, JUST ONCE?
I WISH I HAD AWESOME WINGS LIKE YOURS, ERIS.
AT LEAST WE HAVE REACHED OUR DESTINATION...
LAVAL, ERIS, AND FLINX SOON COME UPON THE SABER-TOOTHED TIGERS AND MAMMOTHS AS THEY ARE BUILDING A HOLIDAY HOME FOR SIR FANGAR...
I THINK IT NEEDS TO BE A BIT FARTHER TO THE RIGHT. AFTER ALL, I WANT TO HAVE A PERFECT VIEW OF MY NEW ICE FLOWER!
THIS IS HUMILIATING! WE'RE MAMMOTHS, NOT SNOW SHOVELS!

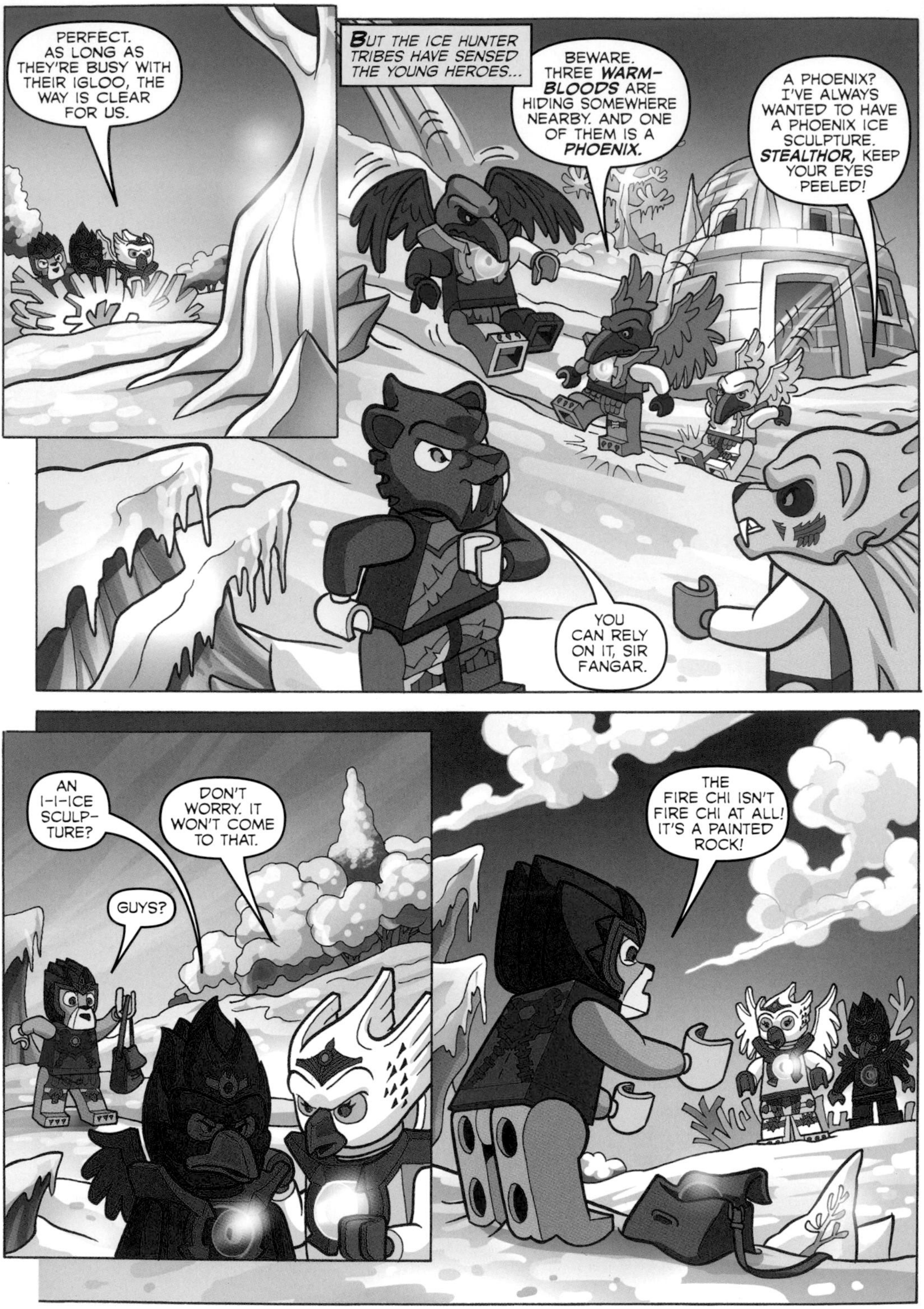
PERFECT. AS LONG AS THEY'RE BUSY WITH THEIR IGLOO, THE WAY IS CLEAR FOR US.
BUT THE ICE HUNTER TRIBES HAVE SENSED THE YOUNG HEROES...
BEWARE. THREE WARM-BLOODS ARE HIDING SOMEWHERE NEARBY. AND ONE OF THEM IS A PHOENIX.
A PHOENIX? I'VE ALWAYS WANTED TO HAVE A PHOENIX ICE SCULPTURE. STEALTHOR, KEEP YOUR EYES PEELED!
YOU CAN RELY ON IT, SIR FANGAR.
AN I-I-ICE SCULP-TURE?
DON'T WORRY. IT WON'T COME TO THAT.
GUYS?
THE FIRE CHI ISN'T FIRE CHI AT ALL! IT'S A PAINTED ROCK!

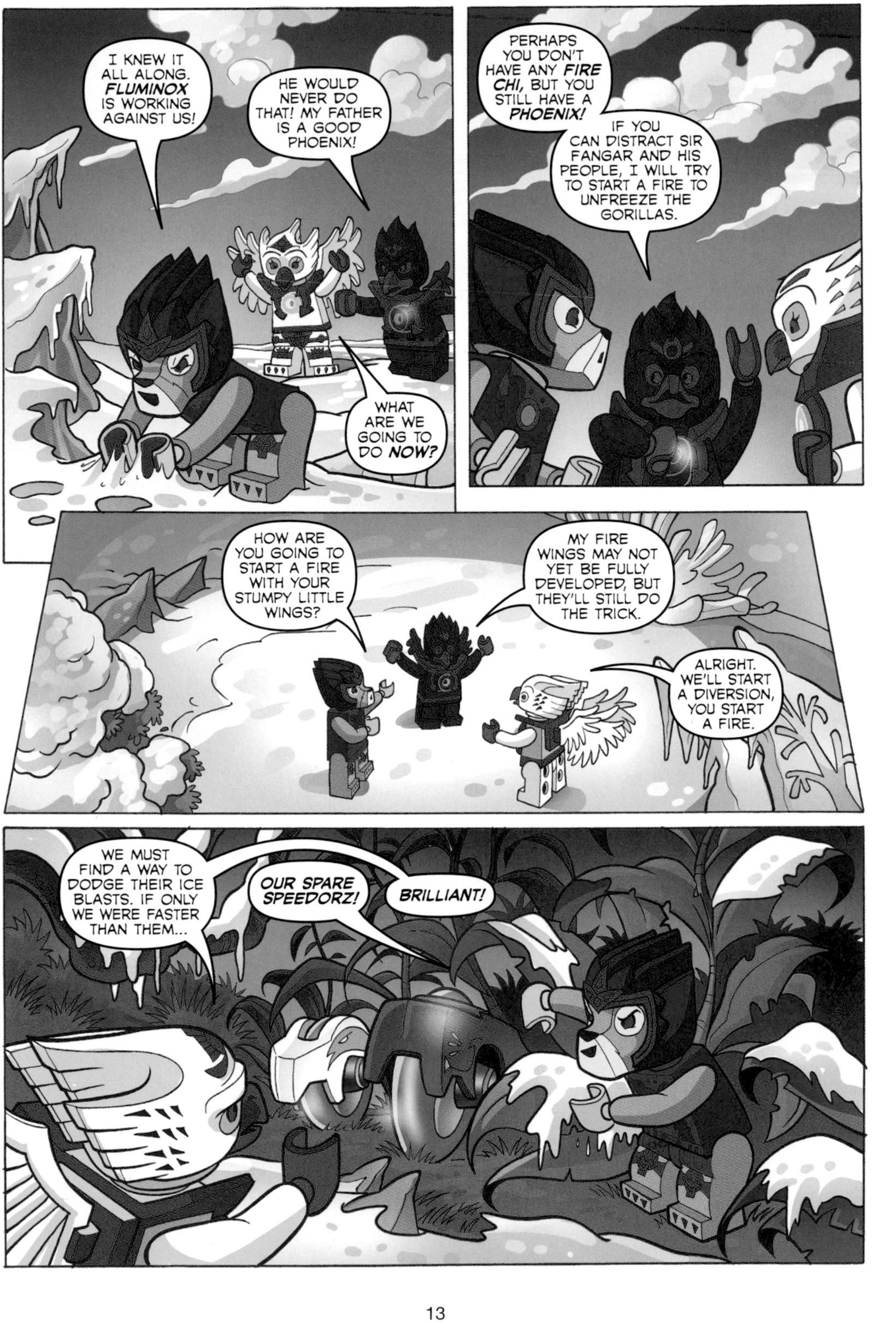
I KNEW IT ALL ALONG. FLUMINOX IS WORKING AGAINST US!
HE WOULD NEVER DO THAT! MY FATHER IS A GOOD PHOENIX!
WHAT ARE WE GOING TO DO NOW?
PERHAPS YOU DON'T HAVE ANY FIRE CHI, BUT YOU STILL HAVE A PHOENIX!
IF YOU CAN DISTRACT SIR FANGAR AND HIS PEOPLE, I WILL TRY TO START A FIRE TO UNFREEZE THE GORILLAS.
HOW ARE YOU GOING TO START A FIRE WITH YOUR STUMPY LITTLE WINGS?
MY FIRE WINGS MAY NOT YET BE FULLY DEVELOPED, BUT THEY'LL STILL DO THE TRICK.
ALRIGHT. WE'LL START A DIVERSION, YOU START A FIRE.
WE MUST FIND A WAY TO DODGE THEIR ICE BLASTS. IF ONLY WE WERE FASTER THAN THEM...
OUR SPARE SPEEDORZ!
BRILLIANT!

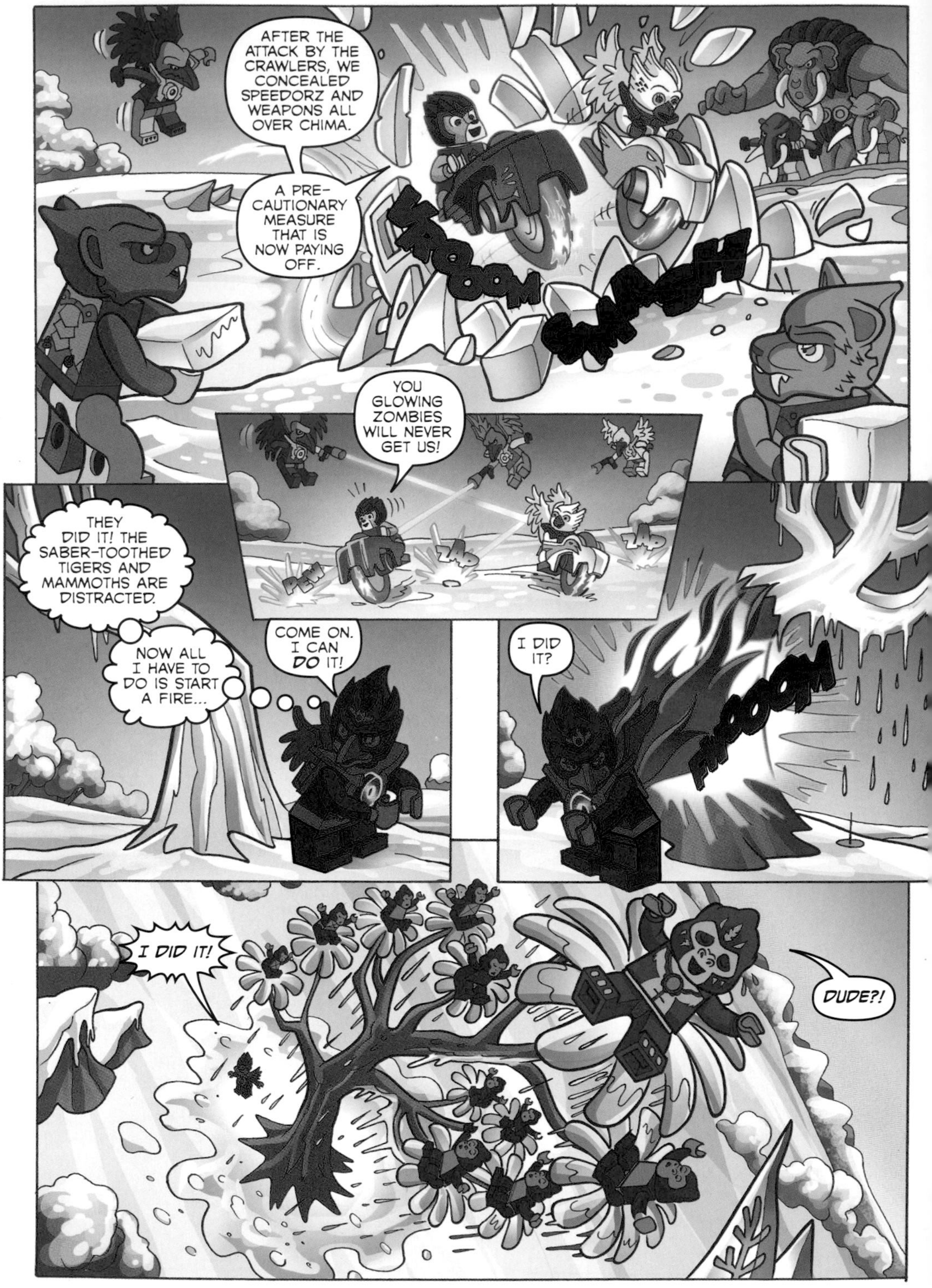
AFTER THE ATTACK BY THE CRAWLERS, WE CONCEALED SPEEDORZ AND WEAPONS ALL OVER CHIMA.
A PRE-CAUTIONARY MEASURE THAT IS NOW PAYING OFF.
VROOOM
SMASH
YOU GLOWING ZOMBIES WILL NEVER GET US!
PEW
ZAP
ZAP
THEY DID IT! THE SABER-TOOTHED TIGERS AND MAMMOTHS ARE DISTRACTED.
NOW ALL I HAVE TO DO IS START A FIRE...
COME ON. I CAN DO IT!
I DID IT?
FWOOOM
I DID IT!
DUDE?!

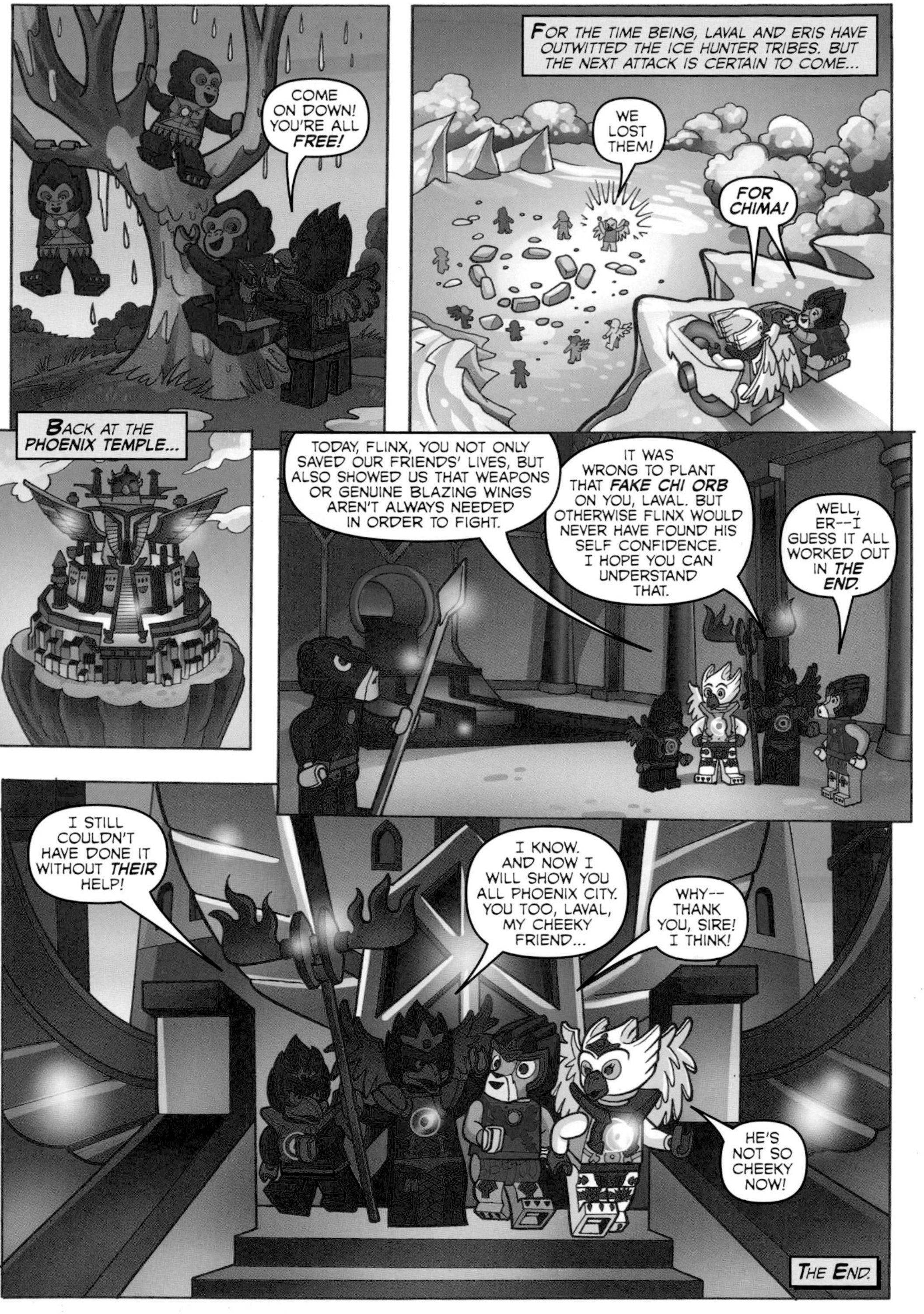
COME ON DOWN! YOU'RE ALL FREE!
FOR THE TIME BEING, LAVAL AND ERIS HAVE OUTWITTED THE ICE HUNTER TRIBES. BUT THE NEXT ATTACK IS CERTAIN TO COME...
WE LOST THEM!
FOR CHIMA!
BACK AT THE PHOENIX TEMPLE...
TODAY, FLINX, YOU NOT ONLY SAVED OUR FRIENDS' LIVES, BUT ALSO SHOWED US THAT WEAPONS OR GENUINE BLAZING WINGS AREN'T ALWAYS NEEDED IN ORDER TO FIGHT.
IT WAS WRONG TO PLANT THAT FAKE CHI ORB ON YOU, LAVAL. BUT OTHERWISE FLINX WOULD NEVER HAVE FOUND HIS SELF CONFIDENCE. I HOPE YOU CAN UNDERSTAND THAT.
WELL, ER--I GUESS IT ALL WORKED OUT IN THE END.
I STILL COULDN'T HAVE DONE IT WITHOUT THEIR HELP!
I KNOW. AND NOW I WILL SHOW YOU ALL PHOENIX CITY. YOU TOO, LAVAL, MY CHEEKY FRIEND...
WHY-- THANK YOU, SIRE! I THINK!
HE'S NOT SO CHEEKY NOW!
THE END.

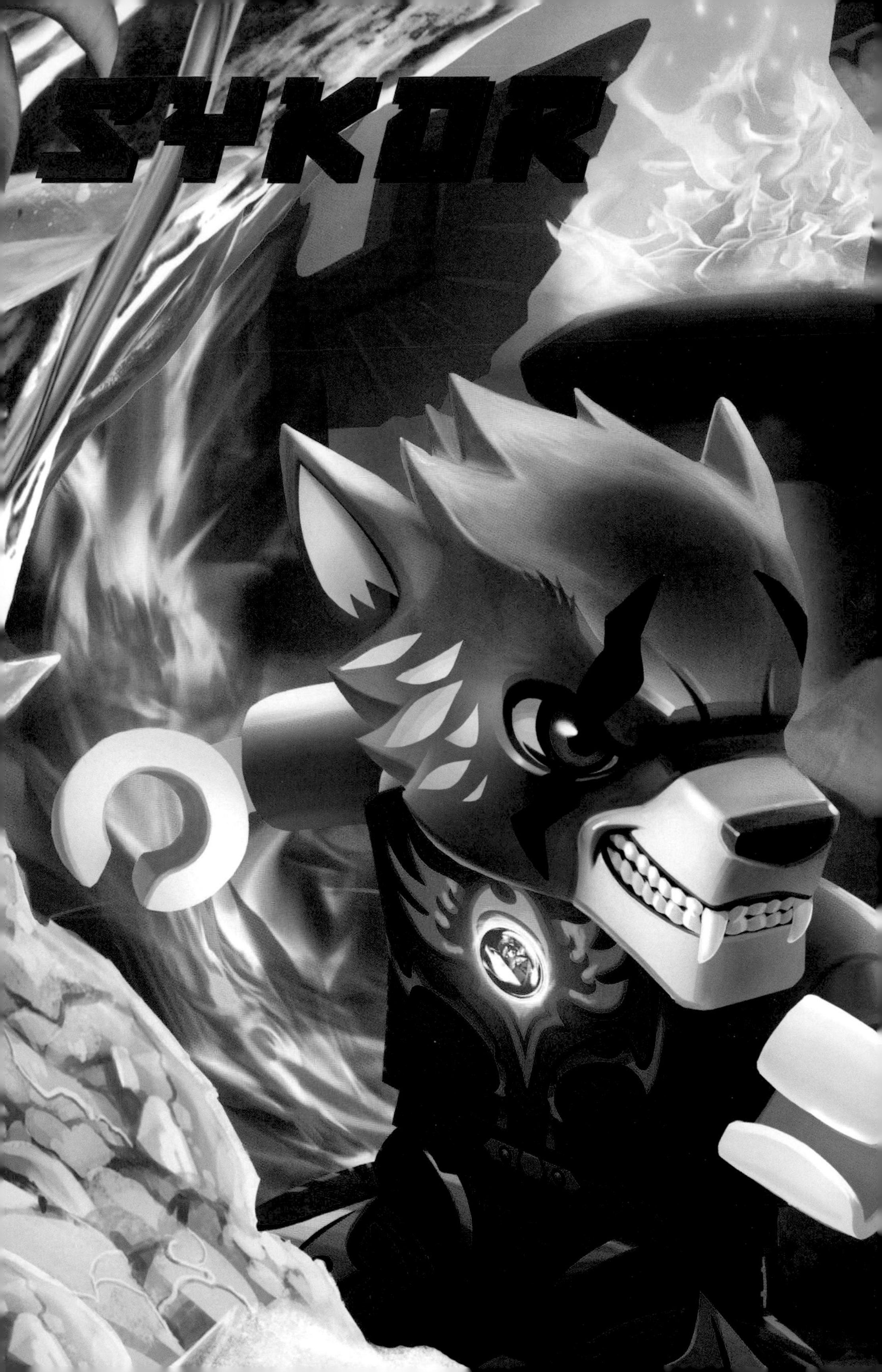
SYKOR

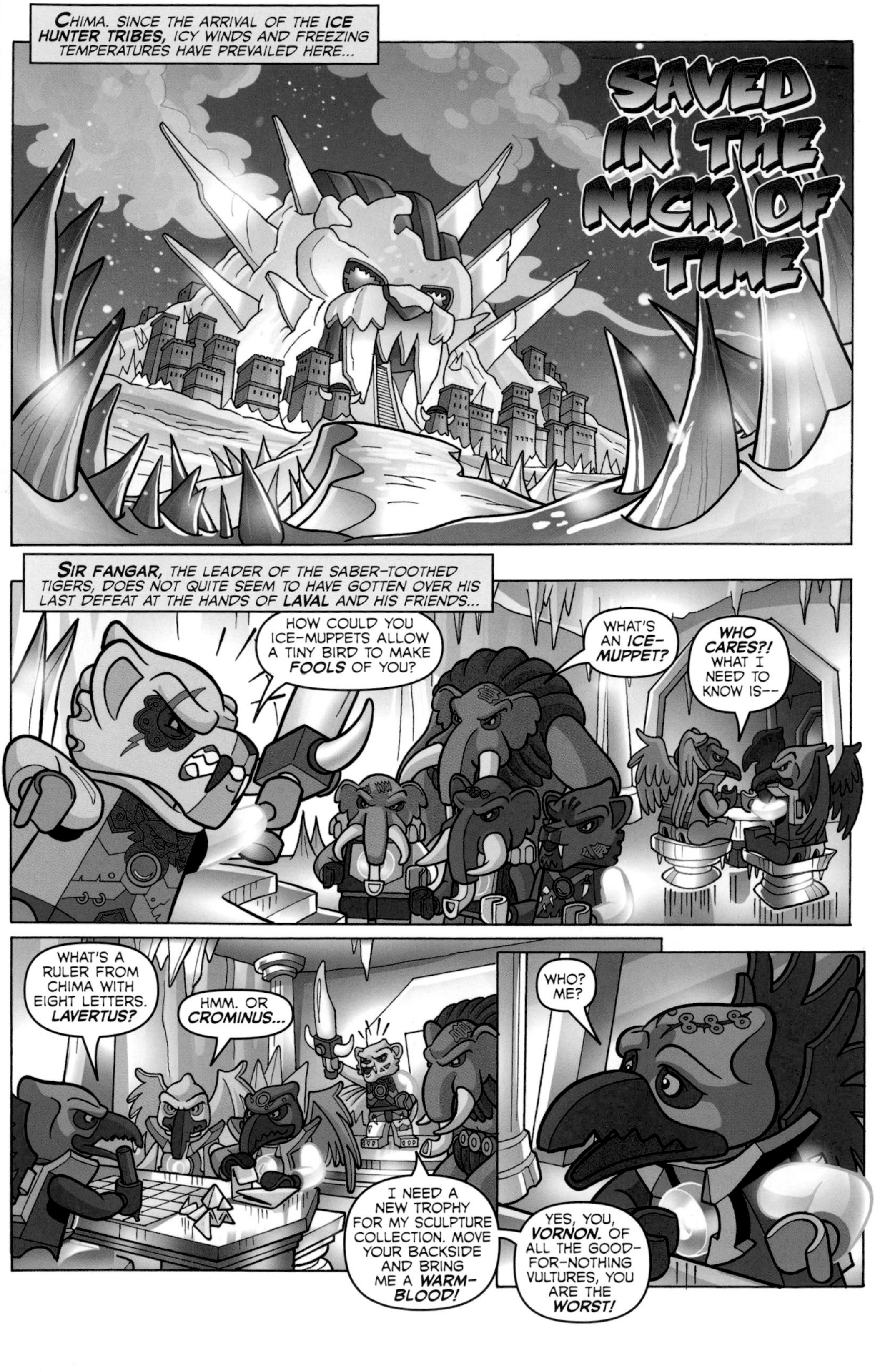
CHIMA. SINCE THE ARRIVAL OF THE ICE HUNTER TRIBES, ICY WINDS AND FREEZING TEMPERATURES HAVE PREVAILED HERE...
SAVED IN THE NICK OF TIME
SIR FANGAR, THE LEADER OF THE SABER-TOOTHED TIGERS, DOES NOT QUITE SEEM TO HAVE GOTTEN OVER HIS LAST DEFEAT AT THE HANDS OF LAVAL AND HIS FRIENDS...
HOW COULD YOU ICE-MUPPETS ALLOW A TINY BIRD TO MAKE FOOLS OF YOU?
WHAT'S AN ICE-MUPPET?
WHO CARES?! WHAT I NEED TO KNOW IS--
WHAT'S A RULER FROM CHIMA WITH EIGHT LETTERS. LAVERTUS?
HMM. OR CROMINUS...
I NEED A NEW TROPHY FOR MY SCULPTURE COLLECTION. MOVE YOUR BACKSIDE AND BRING ME A WARM-BLOOD!
WHO? ME?
YES, YOU, VORNON. OF ALL THE GOOD-FOR-NOTHING VULTURES, YOU ARE THE WORST!

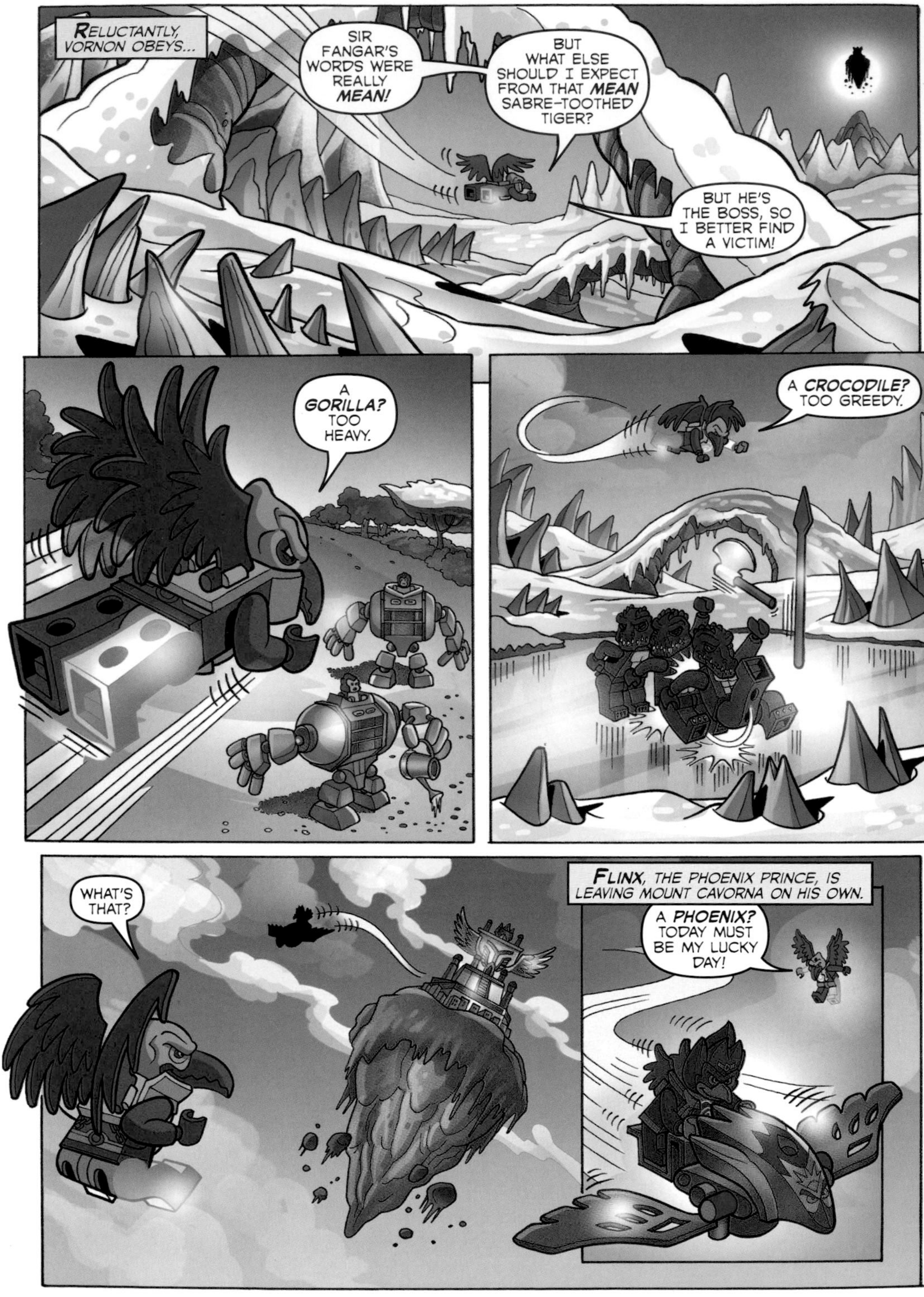
RELUCTANTLY, VORNON OBEYS...
SIR FANGAR'S WORDS WERE REALLY MEAN!
BUT WHAT ELSE SHOULD I EXPECT FROM THAT MEAN SABRE-TOOTHED TIGER?
BUT HE'S THE BOSS, SO I BETTER FIND A VICTIM!
A GORILLA? TOO HEAVY.
A CROCODILE? TOO GREEDY.
WHAT'S THAT?
FLINX, THE PHOENIX PRINCE, IS LEAVING MOUNT CAVORNA ON HIS OWN.
A PHOENIX? TODAY MUST BE MY LUCKY DAY!

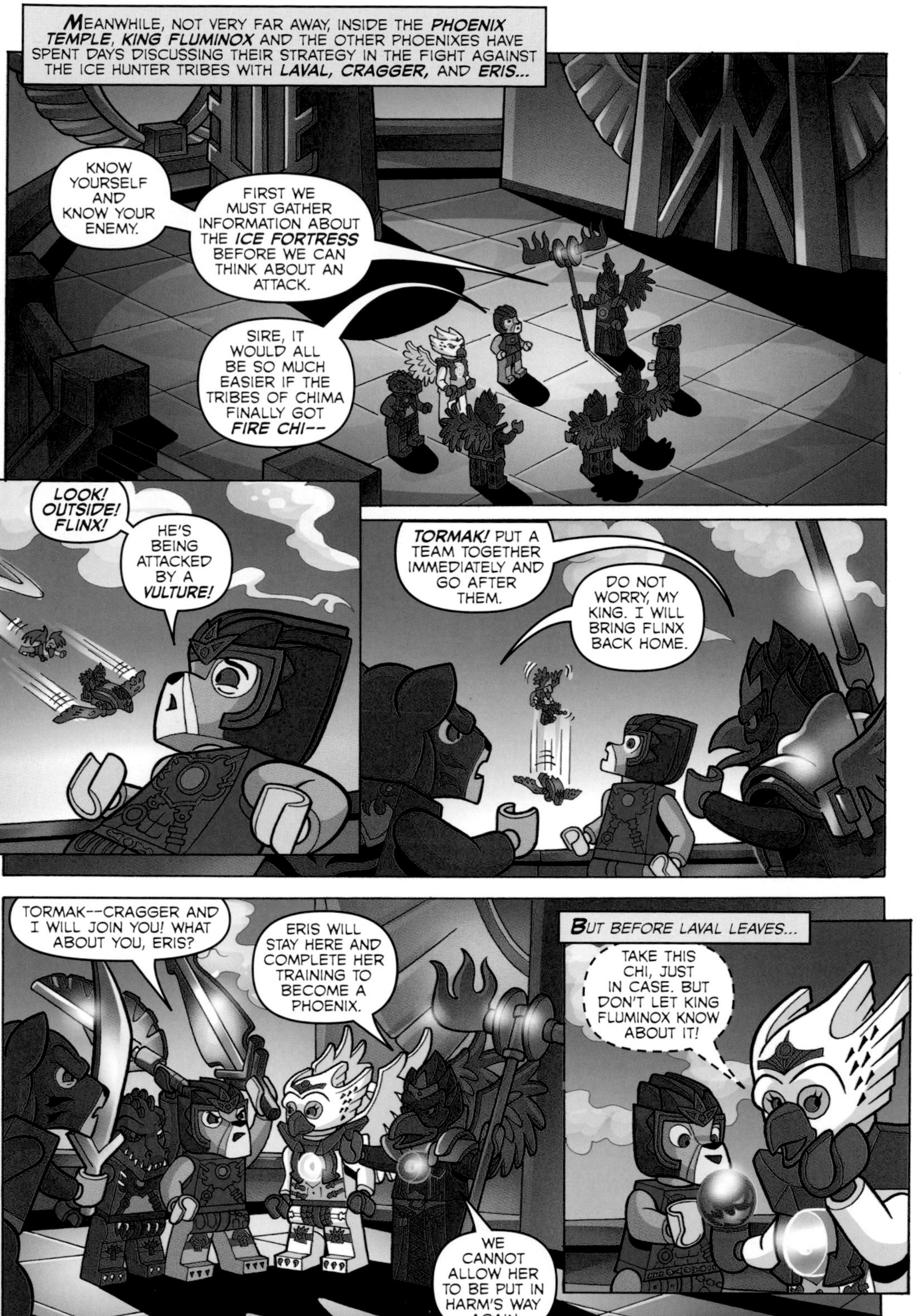
MEANWHILE, NOT VERY FAR AWAY, INSIDE THE PHOENIX TEMPLE, KING FLUMINOX AND THE OTHER PHOENIXES HAVE SPENT DAYS DISCUSSING THEIR STRATEGY IN THE FIGHT AGAINST THE ICE HUNTER TRIBES WITH LAVAL, CRAGGER, AND ERIS...
KNOW YOURSELF AND KNOW YOUR ENEMY.
FIRST WE MUST GATHER INFORMATION ABOUT THE ICE FORTRESS BEFORE WE CAN THINK ABOUT AN ATTACK.
SIRE, IT WOULD ALL BE SO MUCH EASIER IF THE TRIBES OF CHIMA FINALLY GOT FIRE CHI--
LOOK! OUTSIDE! FLINX!
HE'S BEING ATTACKED BY A VULTURE!
TORMAK! PUT A TEAM TOGETHER IMMEDIATELY AND GO AFTER THEM.
DO NOT WORRY, MY KING. I WILL BRING FLINX BACK HOME.
TORMAK--CRAGGER AND I WILL JOIN YOU! WHAT ABOUT YOU, ERIS?
ERIS WILL STAY HERE AND COMPLETE HER TRAINING TO BECOME A PHOENIX.
WE CANNOT ALLOW HER TO BE PUT IN HARM'S WAY AGAIN.
BUT BEFORE LAVAL LEAVES...
TAKE THIS CHI, JUST IN CASE. BUT DON'T LET KING FLUMINOX KNOW ABOUT IT!

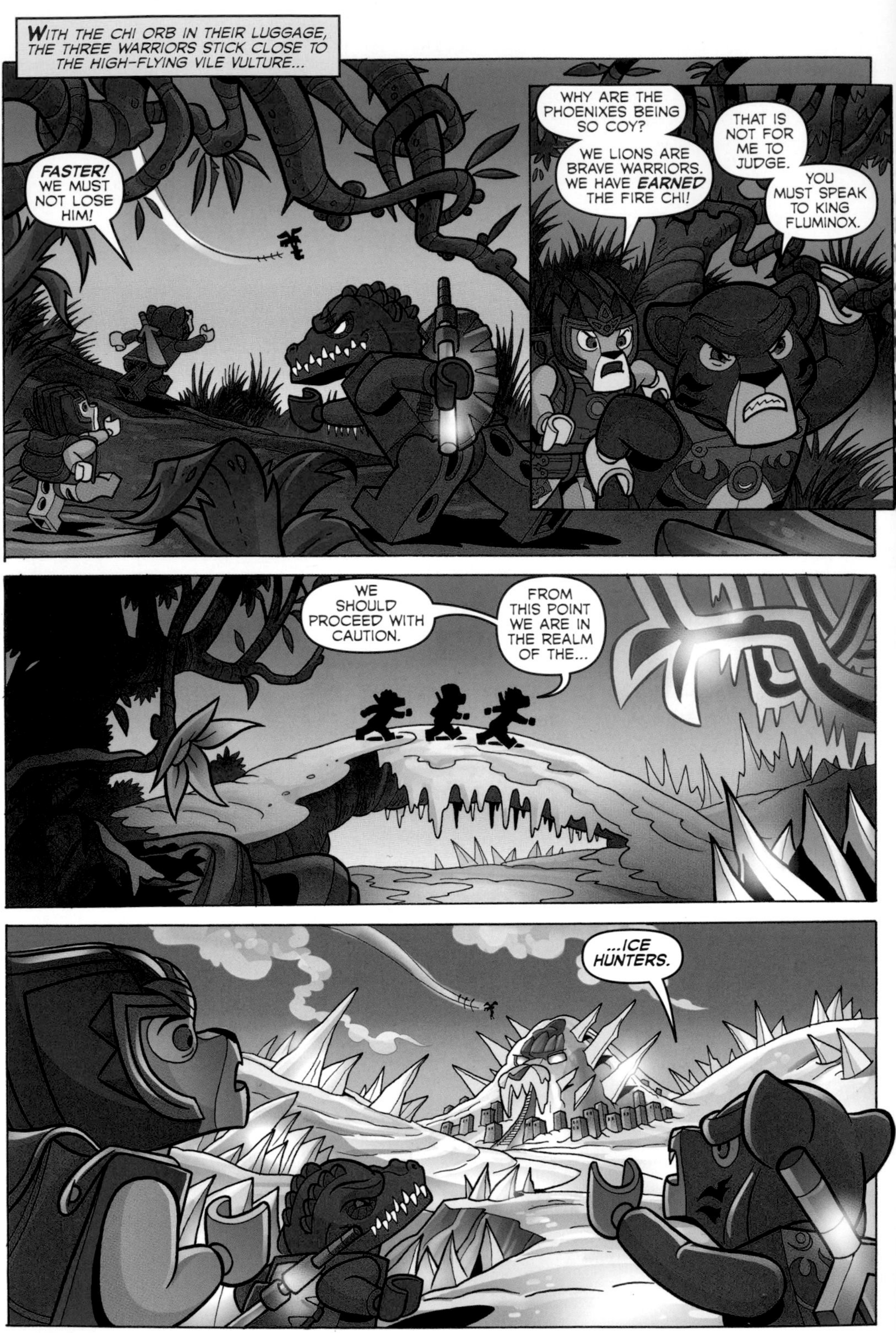
WITH THE CHI ORB IN THEIR LUGGAGE, THE THREE WARRIORS STICK CLOSE TO THE HIGH-FLYING VILE VULTURE...
FASTER! WE MUST NOT LOSE HIM!
WHY ARE THE PHOENIXES BEING SO COY?
WE LIONS ARE BRAVE WARRIORS. WE HAVE EARNED THE FIRE CHI!
THAT IS NOT FOR ME TO JUDGE.
YOU MUST SPEAK TO KING FLUMINOX.
WE SHOULD PROCEED WITH CAUTION.
FROM THIS POINT WE ARE IN THE REALM OF THE...
...ICE HUNTERS.

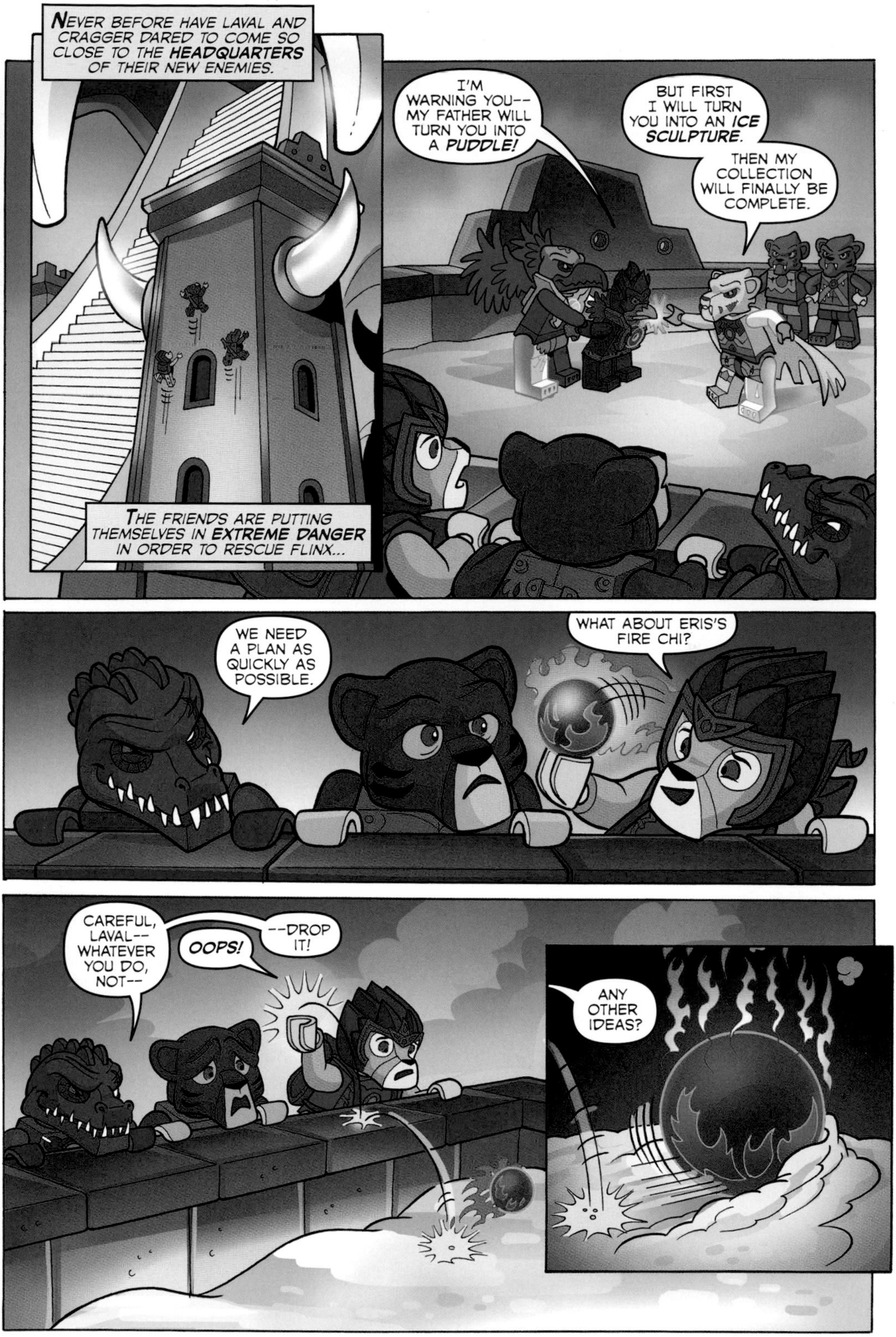
NEVER BEFORE HAVE LAVAL AND CRAGGER DARED TO COME SO CLOSE TO THE HEADQUARTERS OF THEIR NEW ENEMIES.
THE FRIENDS ARE PUTTING THEMSELVES IN EXTREME DANGER IN ORDER TO RESCUE FLINX...
I'M WARNING YOU-- MY FATHER WILL TURN YOU INTO A PUDDLE!
BUT FIRST I WILL TURN YOU INTO AN ICE SCULPTURE.
THEN MY COLLECTION WILL FINALLY BE COMPLETE.
WE NEED A PLAN AS QUICKLY AS POSSIBLE.
WHAT ABOUT ERIS'S FIRE CHI?
CAREFUL, LAVAL-- WHATEVER YOU DO, NOT--
OOPS!
--DROP IT!
ANY OTHER IDEAS?

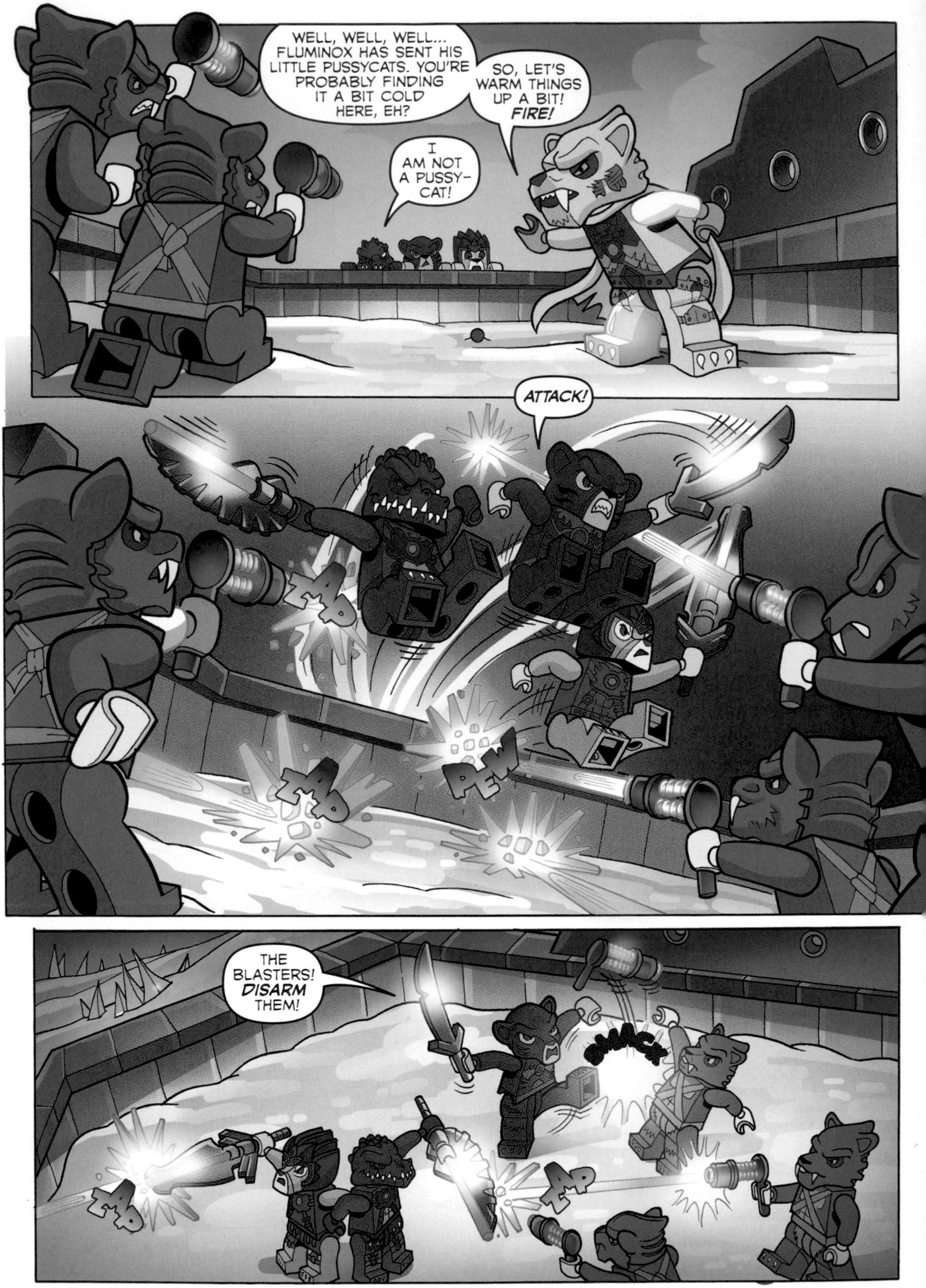

WELL, WELL, WELL... FLUMINOX HAS SENT HIS LITTLE PUSSYCATS. YOU'RE PROBABLY FINDING IT A BIT COLD HERE, EH?
I AM NOT A PUSSY-CAT!
SO, LET'S WARM THINGS UP A BIT! ***FIRE!***
ATTACK!
ZAP
ZAP
PEW
THE BLASTERS! ***DISARM*** THEM!
SMACK
ZAP
ZAP

23

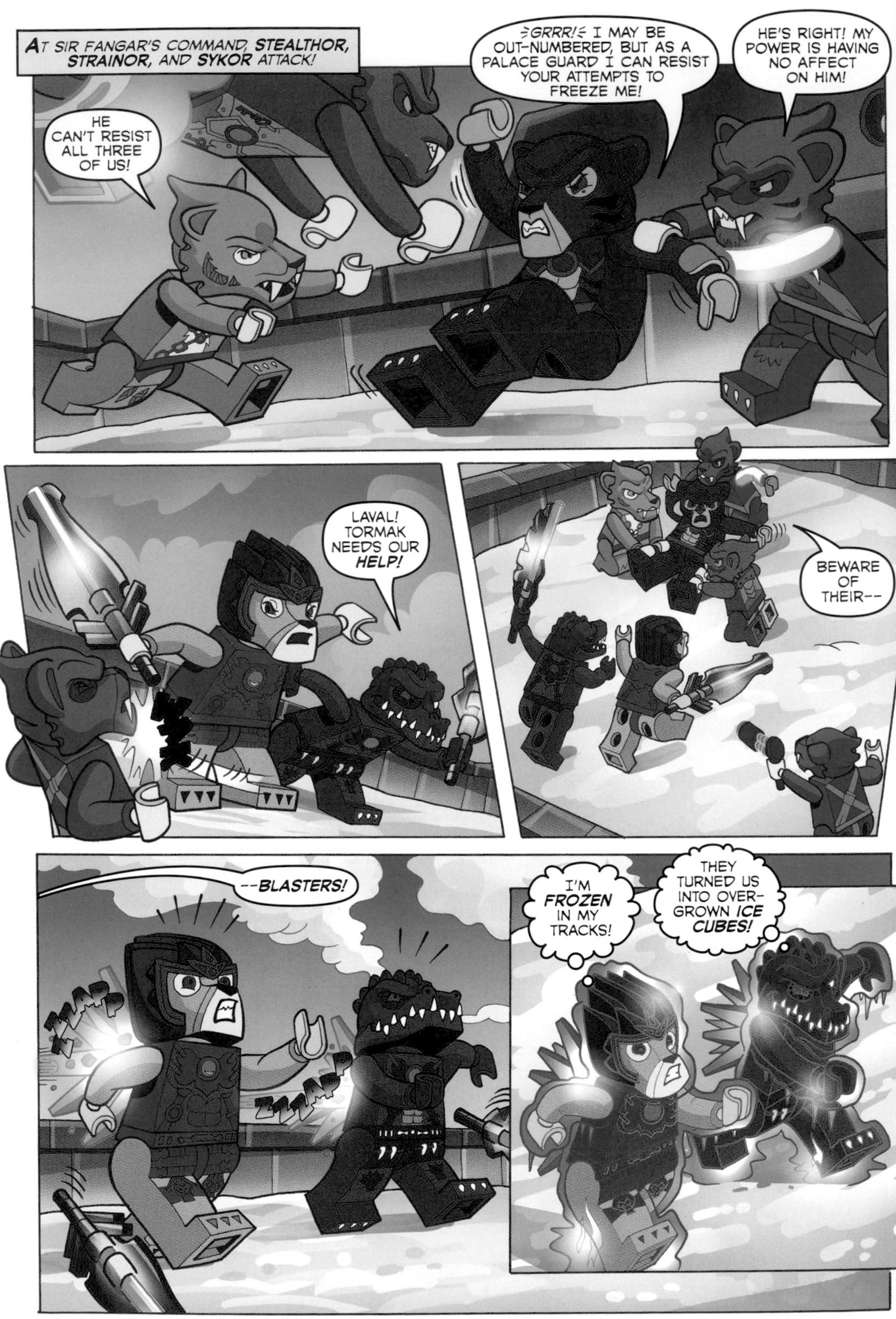
AT SIR FANGAR'S COMMAND, STEALTHOR, STRAINOR, AND SYKOR ATTACK!
HE CAN'T RESIST ALL THREE OF US!
GRRR! I MAY BE OUT-NUMBERED, BUT AS A PALACE GUARD I CAN RESIST YOUR ATTEMPTS TO FREEZE ME!
HE'S RIGHT! MY POWER IS HAVING NO AFFECT ON HIM!
LAVAL! TORMAK NEEDS OUR HELP!
BEWARE OF THEIR--
--BLASTERS!
ZZZAP
I'M FROZEN IN MY TRACKS!
THEY TURNED US INTO OVER-GROWN ICE CUBES!

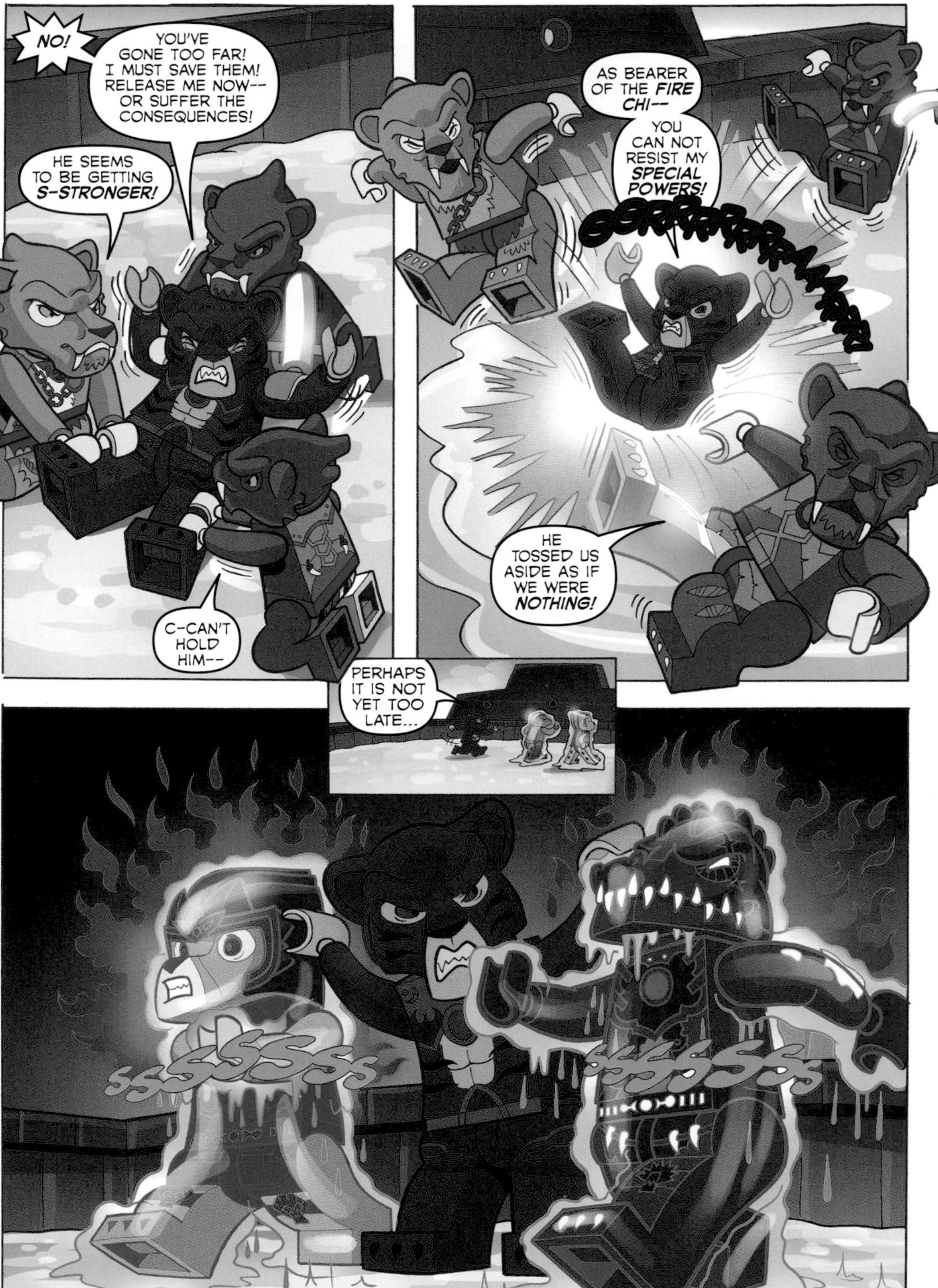
NO!
YOU'VE GONE TOO FAR! I MUST SAVE THEM! RELEASE ME NOW-- OR SUFFER THE CONSEQUENCES!
HE SEEMS TO BE GETTING *S-STRONGER!*
C-CAN'T HOLD HIM--
AS BEARER OF THE *FIRE CHI--*
YOU CAN NOT RESIST MY *SPECIAL POWERS!*
GGRRRRRRRRAAAHRR!
HE TOSSED US ASIDE AS IF WE WERE *NOTHING!*
PERHAPS IT IS NOT YET TOO LATE...
SSSSSSSS
SSSSSSSS

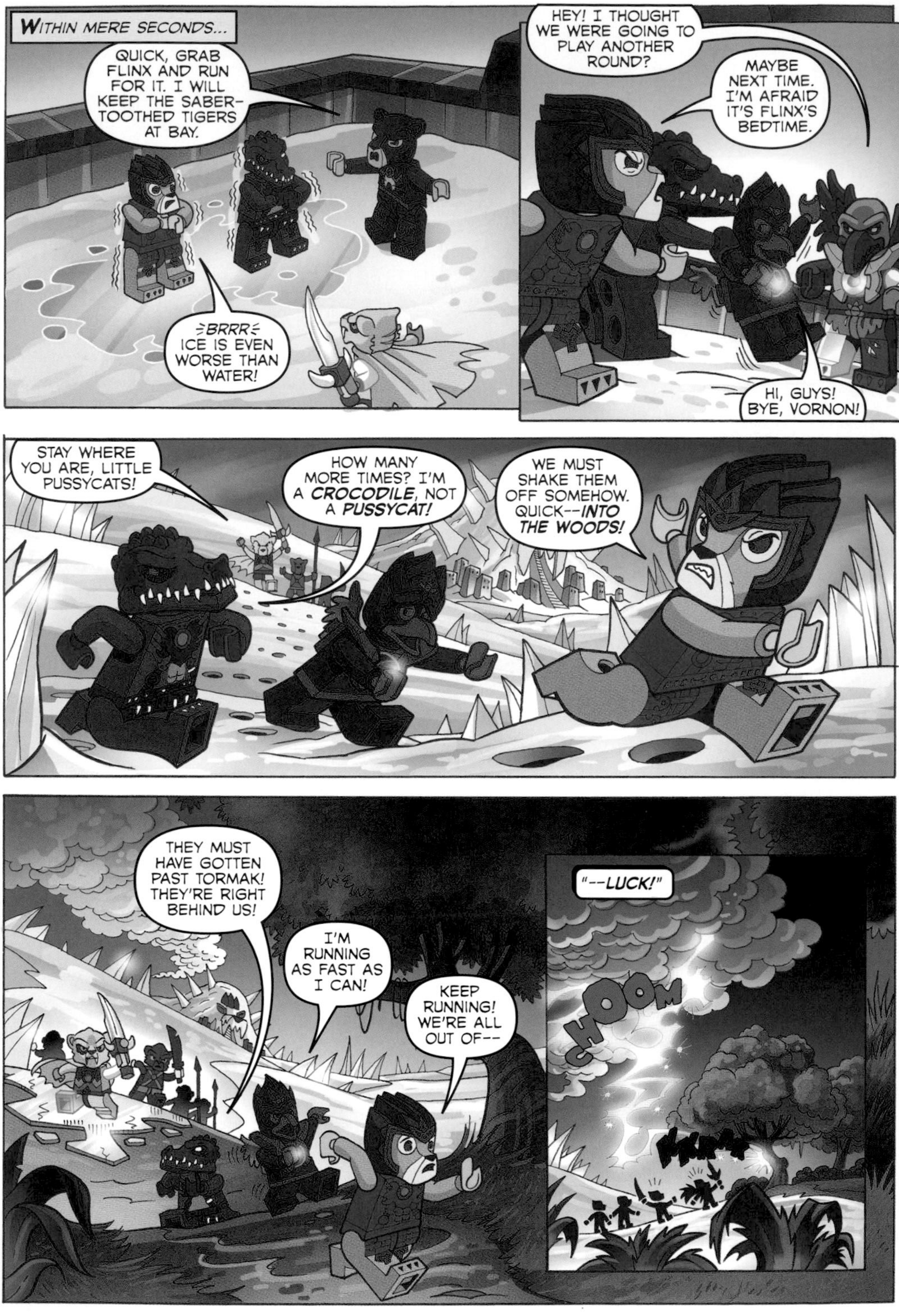
WITHIN MERE SECONDS...
QUICK, GRAB FLINX AND RUN FOR IT. I WILL KEEP THE SABER-TOOTHED TIGERS AT BAY.
BRRR ICE IS EVEN WORSE THAN WATER!
HEY! I THOUGHT WE WERE GOING TO PLAY ANOTHER ROUND?
MAYBE NEXT TIME. I'M AFRAID IT'S FLINX'S BEDTIME.
HI, GUYS! BYE, VORNON!
STAY WHERE YOU ARE, LITTLE PUSSYCATS!
HOW MANY MORE TIMES? I'M A CROCODILE, NOT A PUSSYCAT!
WE MUST SHAKE THEM OFF SOMEHOW. QUICK--INTO THE WOODS!
THEY MUST HAVE GOTTEN PAST TORMAK! THEY'RE RIGHT BEHIND US!
I'M RUNNING AS FAST AS I CAN!
KEEP RUNNING! WE'RE ALL OUT OF--
"--LUCK!"
CHOOM

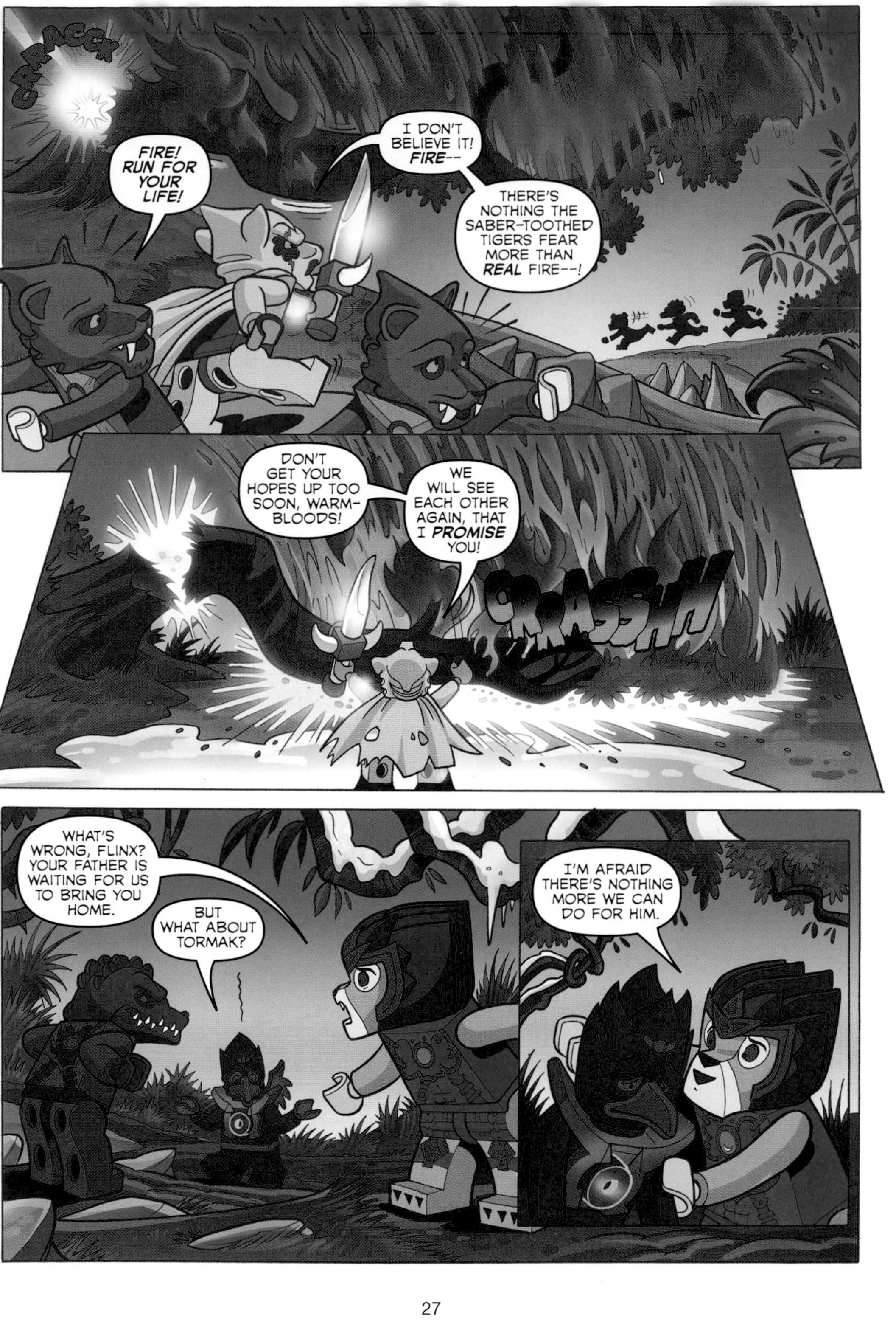
CRACCK
FIRE! RUN FOR YOUR LIFE!
I DON'T BELIEVE IT! FIRE--
THERE'S NOTHING THE SABER-TOOTHED TIGERS FEAR MORE THAN REAL FIRE--!
DON'T GET YOUR HOPES UP TOO SOON, WARM-BLOODS!
WE WILL SEE EACH OTHER AGAIN, THAT I PROMISE YOU!
CRRASSHH
WHAT'S WRONG, FLINX? YOUR FATHER IS WAITING FOR US TO BRING YOU HOME.
BUT WHAT ABOUT TORMAK?
I'M AFRAID THERE'S NOTHING MORE WE CAN DO FOR HIM.

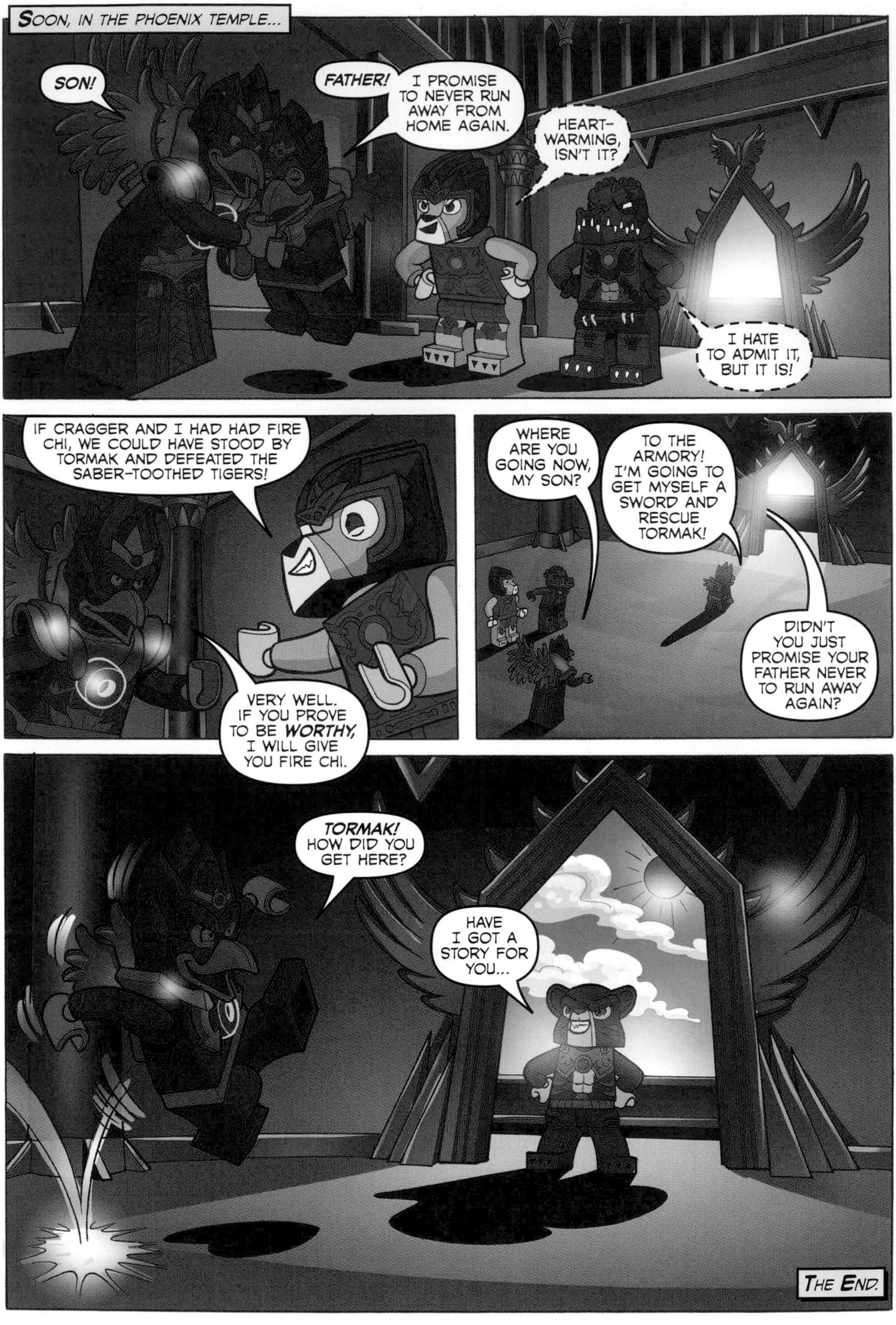
SOON, IN THE PHOENIX TEMPLE...
SON!
FATHER!
I PROMISE TO NEVER RUN AWAY FROM HOME AGAIN.
HEART-WARMING, ISN'T IT?
I HATE TO ADMIT IT, BUT IT IS!
IF CRAGGER AND I HAD HAD FIRE CHI, WE COULD HAVE STOOD BY TORMAK AND DEFEATED THE SABER-TOOTHED TIGERS!
VERY WELL. IF YOU PROVE TO BE WORTHY, I WILL GIVE YOU FIRE CHI.
WHERE ARE YOU GOING NOW, MY SON?
TO THE ARMORY! I'M GOING TO GET MYSELF A SWORD AND RESCUE TORMAK!
DIDN'T YOU JUST PROMISE YOUR FATHER NEVER TO RUN AWAY AGAIN?
TORMAK! HOW DID YOU GET HERE?
HAVE I GOT A STORY FOR YOU...
THE END.

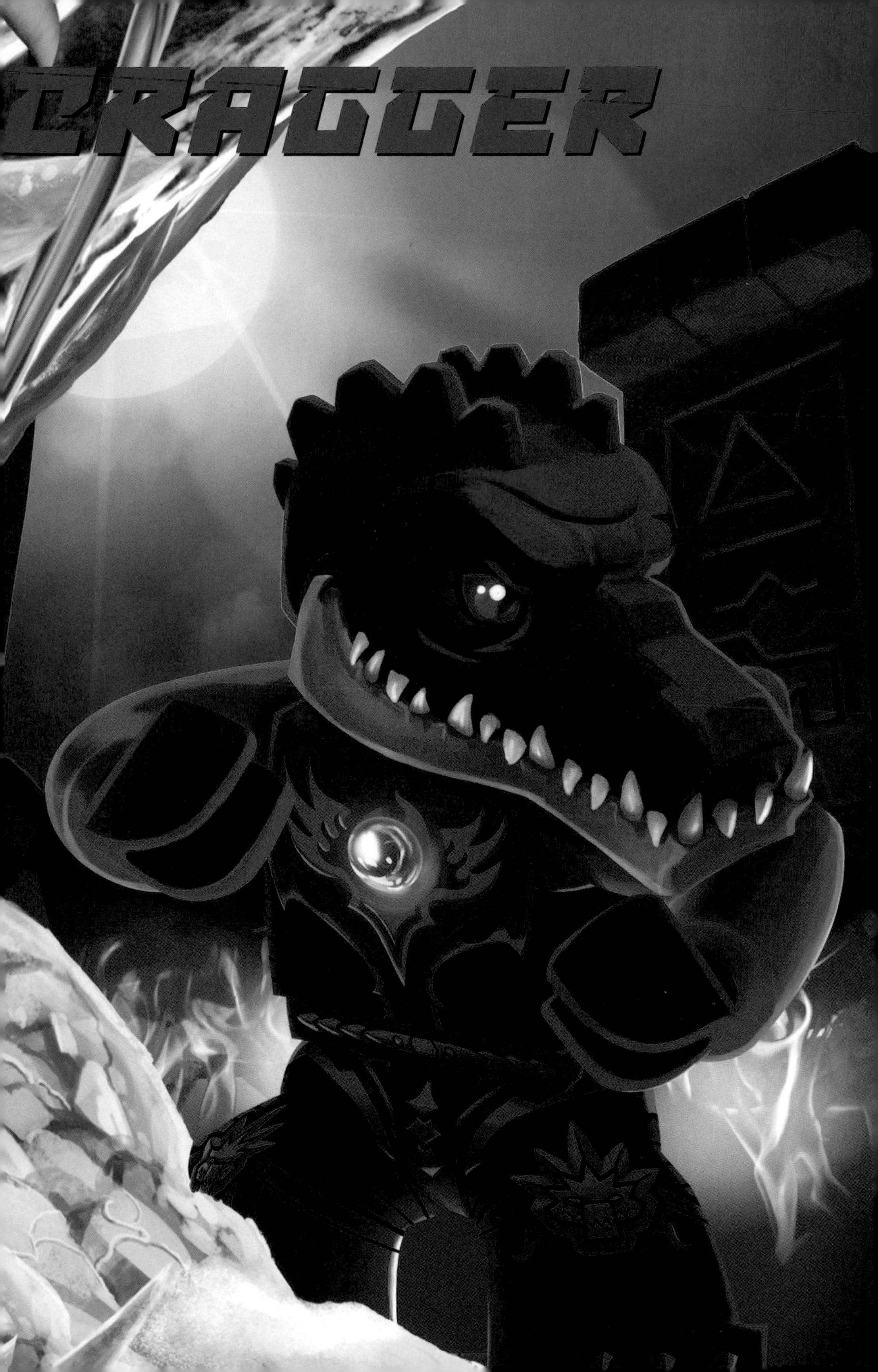
CRAGGER

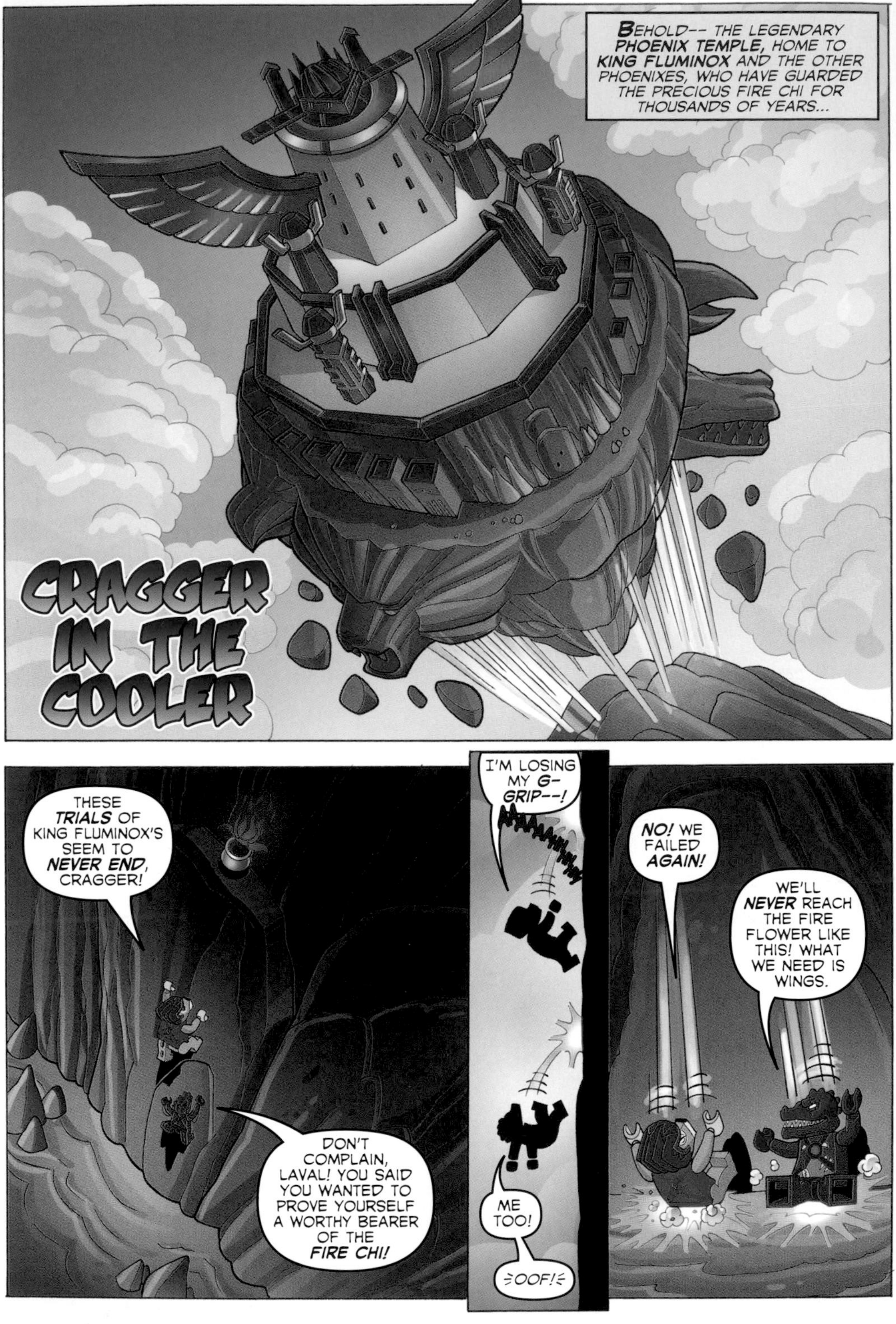
BEHOLD-- THE LEGENDARY PHOENIX TEMPLE, HOME TO KING FLUMINOX AND THE OTHER PHOENIXES, WHO HAVE GUARDED THE PRECIOUS FIRE CHI FOR THOUSANDS OF YEARS...
CRAGGER IN THE COOLER
THESE TRIALS OF KING FLUMINOX'S SEEM TO NEVER END, CRAGGER!
DON'T COMPLAIN, LAVAL! YOU WANTED TO PROVE YOURSELF A WORTHY BEARER OF THE FIRE CHI!
I'M LOSING MY G-GRIP--!
ME TOO!
OOF!
NO! WE FAILED AGAIN!
WE'LL NEVER REACH THE FIRE FLOWER LIKE THIS! WHAT WE NEED IS WINGS.

STILL FALLING AT THE FIRST HURDLE? IT'S CHILD'S PLAY!
LI'ELLA?!
HOW DID THE BIG CATS MANAGE TO PASS THE TEST?
I'LL GIVE YOU A TIP.
SOMETIMES YOU HAVE TO IMPROVISE TO REACH YOUR GOAL.
COME ON, CRAGGER. LET'S HAVE ANOTHER TRY.
I'VE HAD ENOUGH. I'M GOING BACK TO MY SWAMP.
YOU CAN'T JUST GIVE UP LIKE THAT!
ACCEPT IT, LAVAL. LIONS AND CROCODILES WILL NEVER BE ABLE TO FLY.
CRAGGER ...?
SORRY, LAVAL! I'M *DONE!*

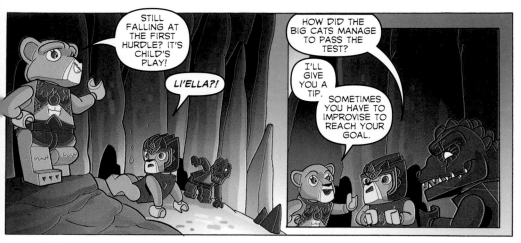

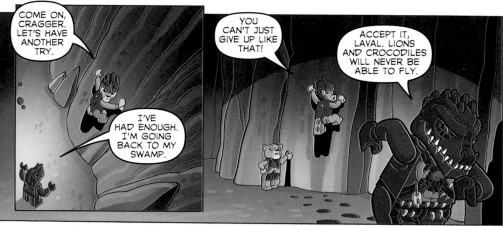

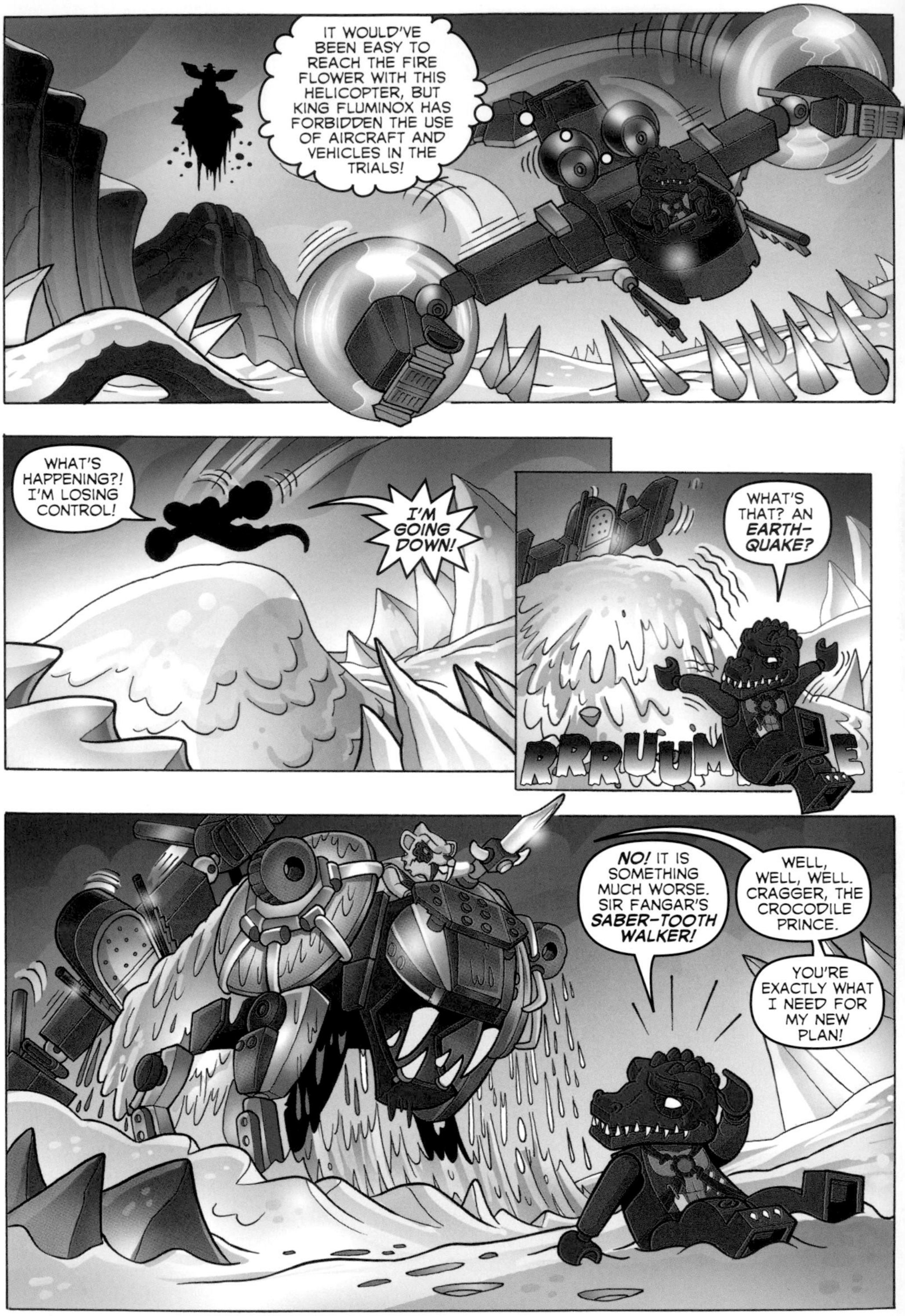
IT WOULD'VE BEEN EASY TO REACH THE FIRE FLOWER WITH THIS HELICOPTER, BUT KING FLUMINOX HAS FORBIDDEN THE USE OF AIRCRAFT AND VEHICLES IN THE TRIALS!
WHAT'S HAPPENING?! I'M LOSING CONTROL!
I'M GOING DOWN!
WHAT'S THAT? AN EARTH-QUAKE?
RRRUUM
NO! IT IS SOMETHING MUCH WORSE. SIR FANGAR'S SABER-TOOTH WALKER!
WELL, WELL, WELL. CRAGGER, THE CROCODILE PRINCE.
YOU'RE EXACTLY WHAT I NEED FOR MY NEW PLAN!

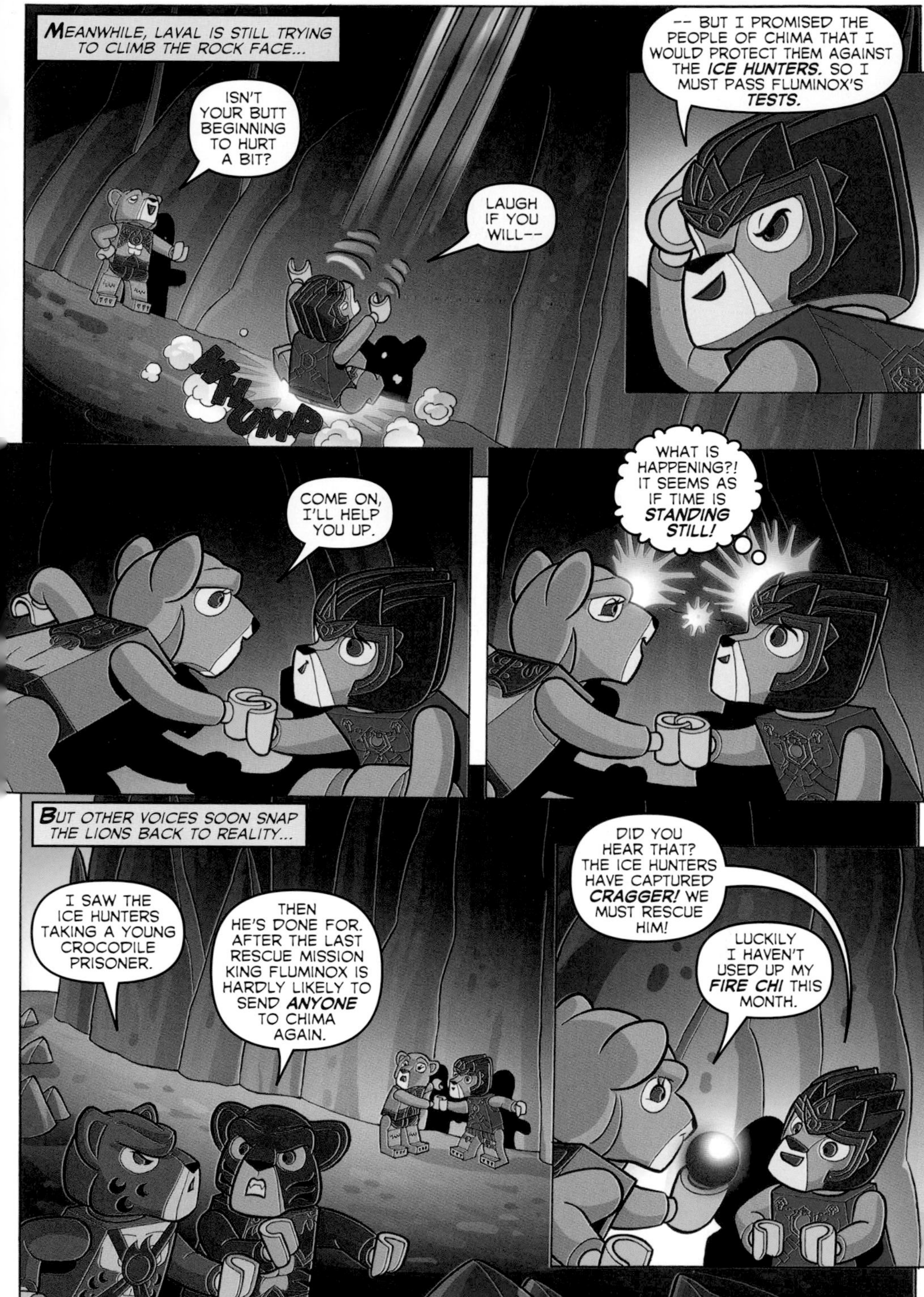
MEANWHILE, LAVAL IS STILL TRYING TO CLIMB THE ROCK FACE...
ISN'T YOUR BUTT BEGINNING TO HURT A BIT?
LAUGH IF YOU WILL--
WHUMP
-- BUT I PROMISED THE PEOPLE OF CHIMA THAT I WOULD PROTECT THEM AGAINST THE ICE HUNTERS. SO I MUST PASS FLUMINOX'S TESTS.
COME ON, I'LL HELP YOU UP.
WHAT IS HAPPENING?! IT SEEMS AS IF TIME IS STANDING STILL!
BUT OTHER VOICES SOON SNAP THE LIONS BACK TO REALITY...
I SAW THE ICE HUNTERS TAKING A YOUNG CROCODILE PRISONER.
THEN HE'S DONE FOR. AFTER THE LAST RESCUE MISSION KING FLUMINOX IS HARDLY LIKELY TO SEND ANYONE TO CHIMA AGAIN.
DID YOU HEAR THAT? THE ICE HUNTERS HAVE CAPTURED CRAGGER! WE MUST RESCUE HIM!
LUCKILY I HAVEN'T USED UP MY FIRE CHI THIS MONTH.

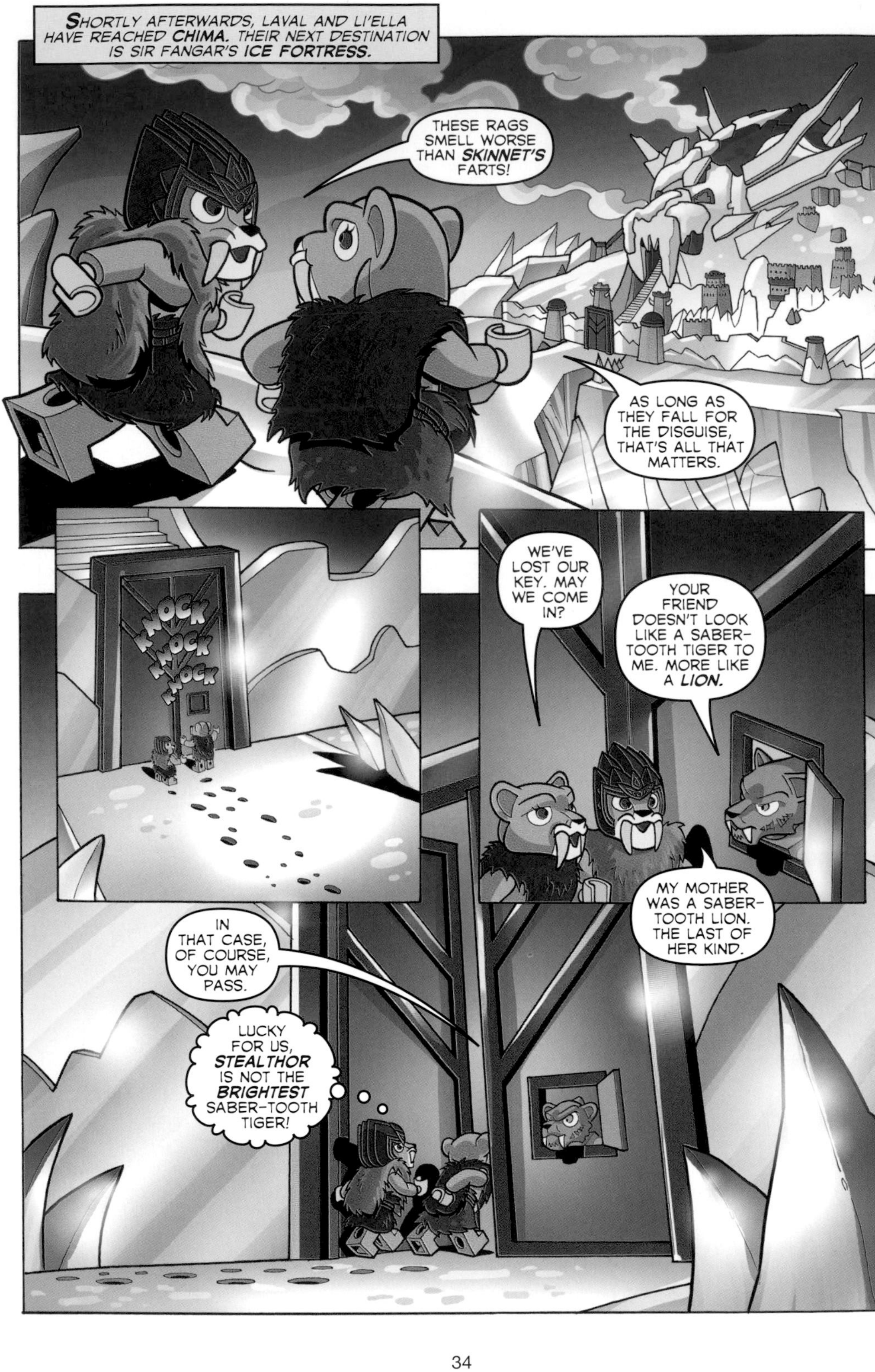
SHORTLY AFTERWARDS, LAVAL AND LI'ELLA HAVE REACHED CHIMA. THEIR NEXT DESTINATION IS SIR FANGAR'S ICE FORTRESS.
THESE RAGS SMELL WORSE THAN SKINNET'S FARTS!
AS LONG AS THEY FALL FOR THE DISGUISE, THAT'S ALL THAT MATTERS.
KNOCK KNOCK KNOCK KNOCK
WE'VE LOST OUR KEY. MAY WE COME IN?
YOUR FRIEND DOESN'T LOOK LIKE A SABER-TOOTH TIGER TO ME. MORE LIKE A LION.
MY MOTHER WAS A SABER-TOOTH LION. THE LAST OF HER KIND.
IN THAT CASE, OF COURSE, YOU MAY PASS.
LUCKY FOR US, STEALTHOR IS NOT THE BRIGHTEST SABER-TOOTH TIGER!

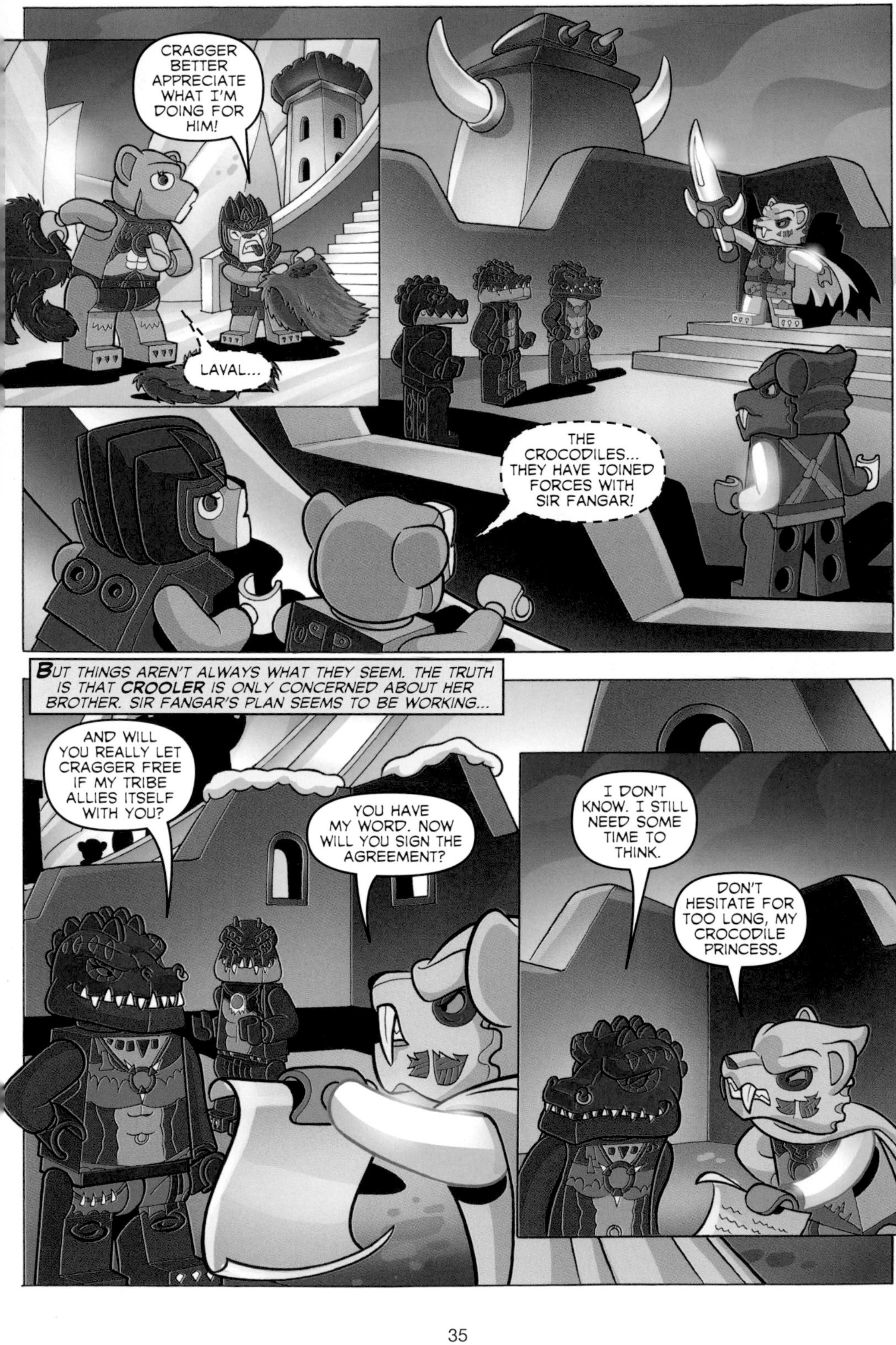
CRAGGER BETTER APPRECIATE WHAT I'M DOING FOR HIM!
LAVAL...
THE CROCODILES... THEY HAVE JOINED FORCES WITH SIR FANGAR!
BUT THINGS AREN'T ALWAYS WHAT THEY SEEM. THE TRUTH IS THAT CROOLER IS ONLY CONCERNED ABOUT HER BROTHER. SIR FANGAR'S PLAN SEEMS TO BE WORKING...
AND WILL YOU REALLY LET CRAGGER FREE IF MY TRIBE ALLIES ITSELF WITH YOU?
YOU HAVE MY WORD. NOW WILL YOU SIGN THE AGREEMENT?
I DON'T KNOW. I STILL NEED SOME TIME TO THINK.
DON'T HESITATE FOR TOO LONG, MY CROCODILE PRINCESS.

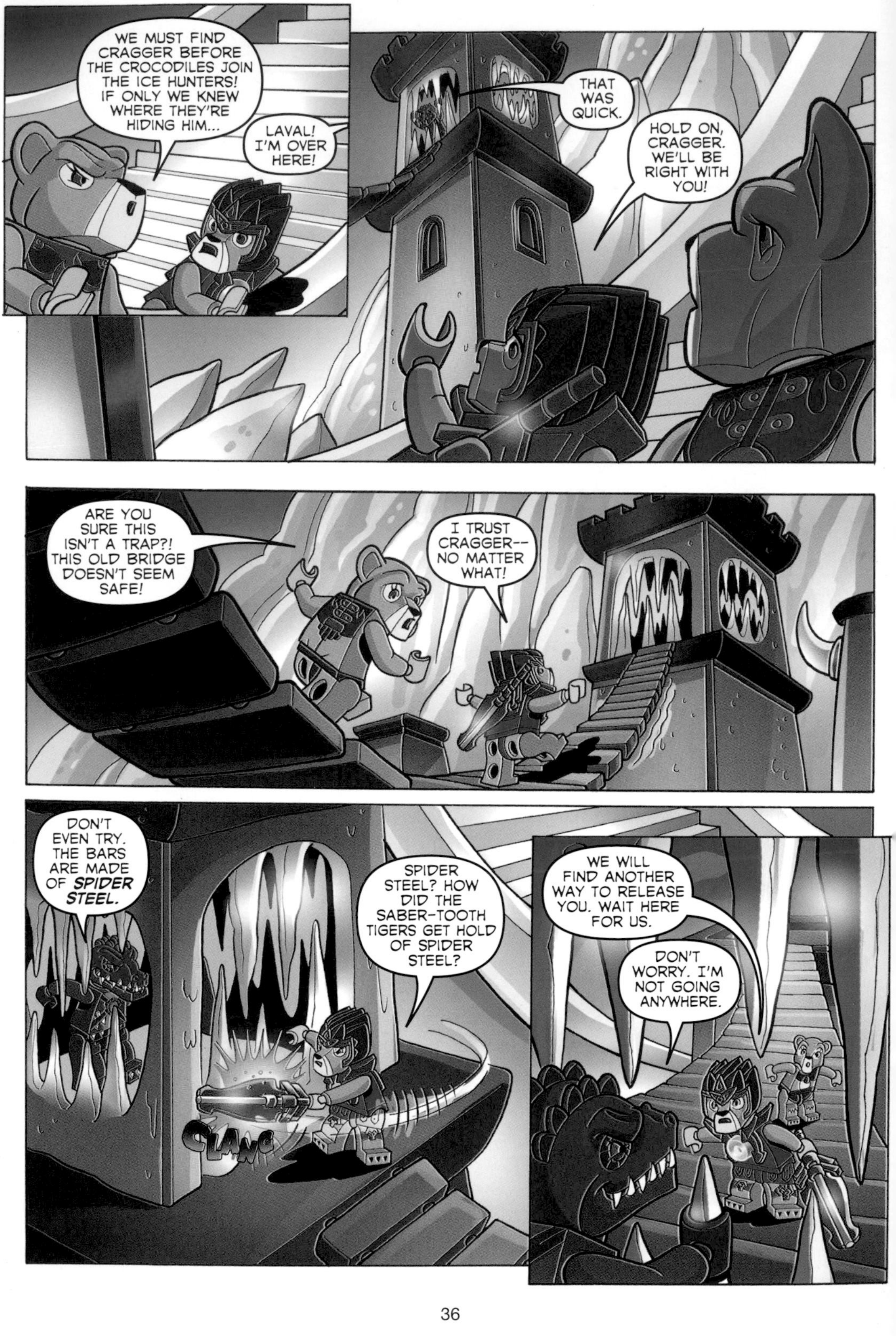
WE MUST FIND CRAGGER BEFORE THE CROCODILES JOIN THE ICE HUNTERS! IF ONLY WE KNEW WHERE THEY'RE HIDING HIM...
LAVAL! I'M OVER HERE!
THAT WAS QUICK.
HOLD ON, CRAGGER. WE'LL BE RIGHT WITH YOU!
ARE YOU SURE THIS ISN'T A TRAP?! THIS OLD BRIDGE DOESN'T SEEM SAFE!
I TRUST CRAGGER-- NO MATTER WHAT!
DON'T EVEN TRY. THE BARS ARE MADE OF ***SPIDER STEEL.***
SPIDER STEEL? HOW DID THE SABER-TOOTH TIGERS GET HOLD OF SPIDER STEEL?
CLANG
WE WILL FIND ANOTHER WAY TO RELEASE YOU. WAIT HERE FOR US.
DON'T WORRY. I'M NOT GOING ANYWHERE.

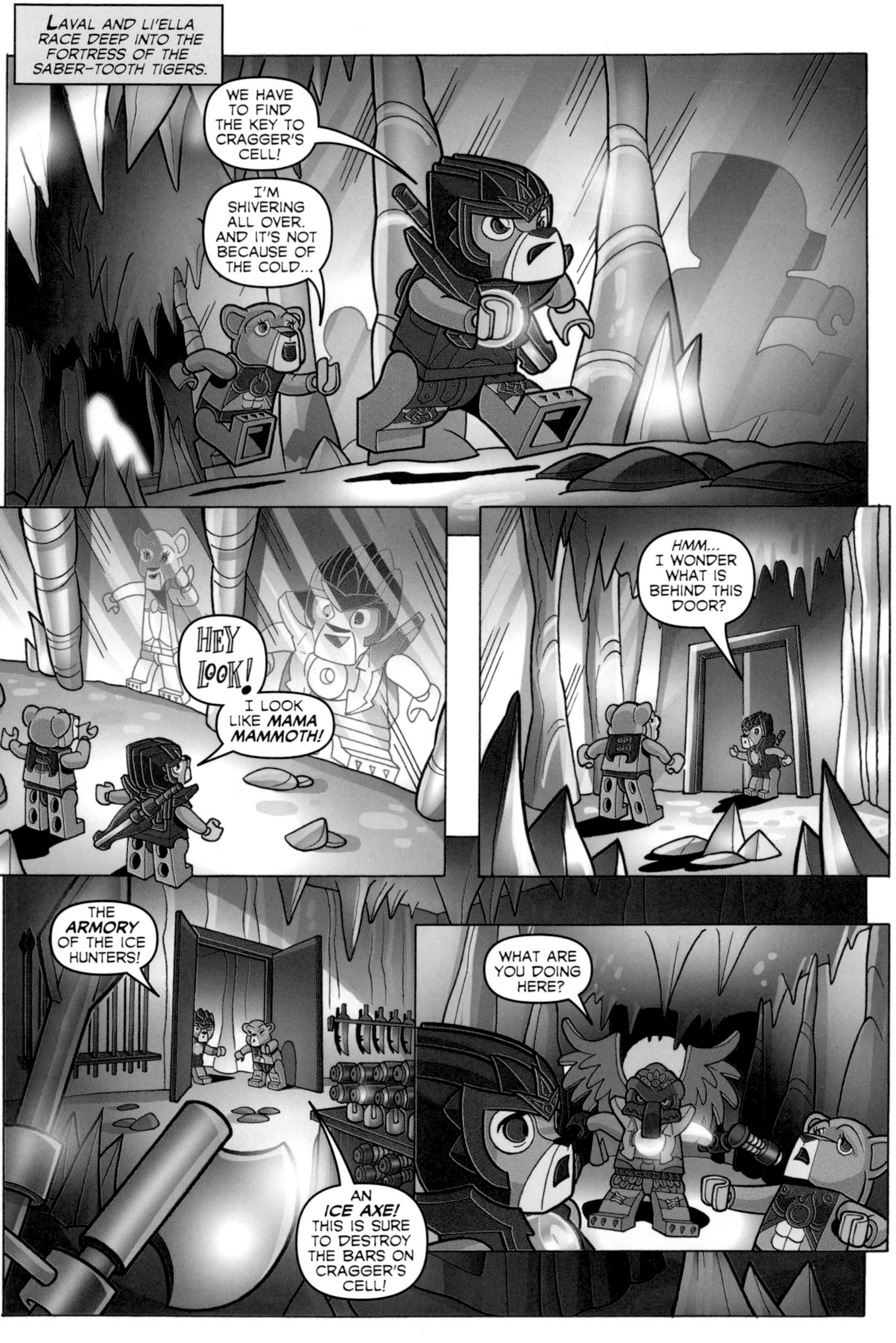
LAVAL AND LI'ELLA RACE DEEP INTO THE FORTRESS OF THE SABER-TOOTH TIGERS.
WE HAVE TO FIND THE KEY TO CRAGGER'S CELL!
I'M SHIVERING ALL OVER. AND IT'S NOT BECAUSE OF THE COLD...
HEY LOOK!
I LOOK LIKE *MAMA MAMMOTH!*
HMM... I WONDER WHAT IS BEHIND THIS DOOR?
THE *ARMORY* OF THE ICE HUNTERS!
AN *ICE AXE!* THIS IS SURE TO DESTROY THE BARS ON CRAGGER'S CELL!
WHAT ARE YOU DOING HERE?

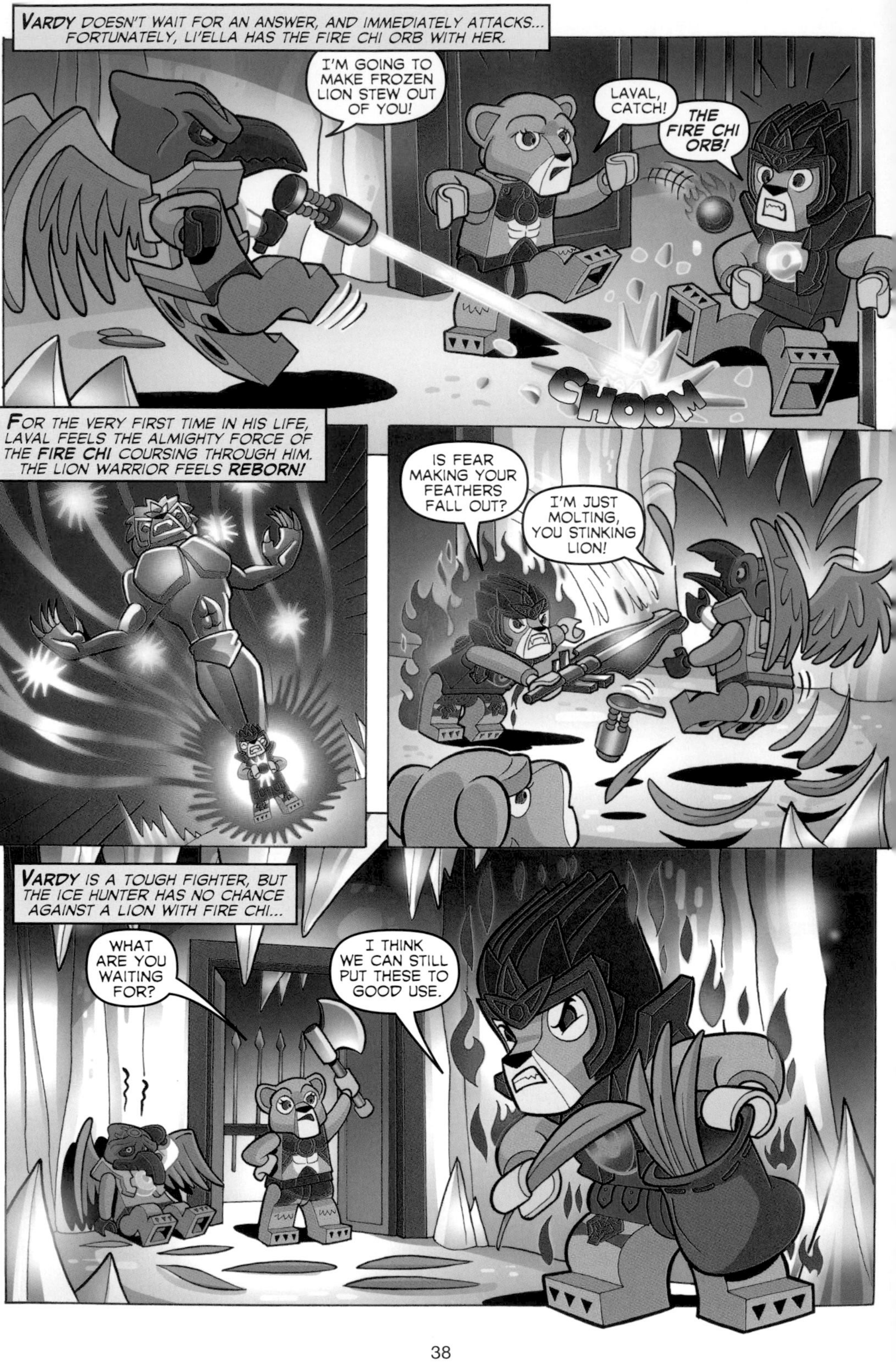
VARDY DOESN'T WAIT FOR AN ANSWER, AND IMMEDIATELY ATTACKS... FORTUNATELY, LI'ELLA HAS THE FIRE CHI ORB WITH HER.
I'M GOING TO MAKE FROZEN LION STEW OUT OF YOU!
LAVAL, CATCH!
THE FIRE CHI ORB!
CHOOM
FOR THE VERY FIRST TIME IN HIS LIFE, LAVAL FEELS THE ALMIGHTY FORCE OF THE FIRE CHI COURSING THROUGH HIM. THE LION WARRIOR FEELS REBORN!
IS FEAR MAKING YOUR FEATHERS FALL OUT?
I'M JUST MOLTING, YOU STINKING LION!
VARDY IS A TOUGH FIGHTER, BUT THE ICE HUNTER HAS NO CHANCE AGAINST A LION WITH FIRE CHI...
WHAT ARE YOU WAITING FOR?
I THINK WE CAN STILL PUT THESE TO GOOD USE.

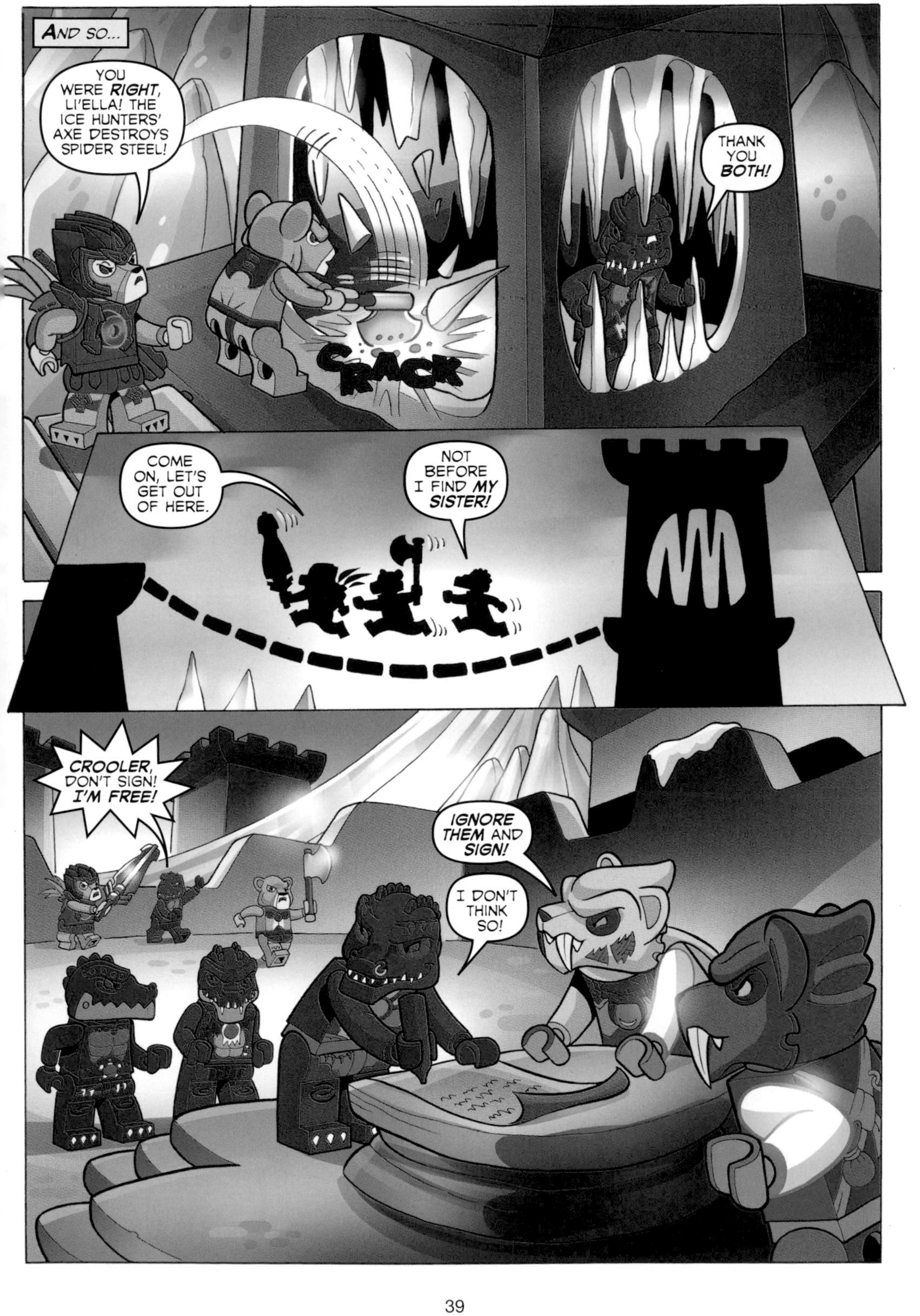
AND SO...
YOU WERE RIGHT, LI'ELLA! THE ICE HUNTERS' AXE DESTROYS SPIDER STEEL!
THANK YOU BOTH!
CRACK
COME ON, LET'S GET OUT OF HERE.
NOT BEFORE I FIND MY SISTER!
CROOLER, DON'T SIGN! I'M FREE!
IGNORE THEM AND SIGN!
I DON'T THINK SO!

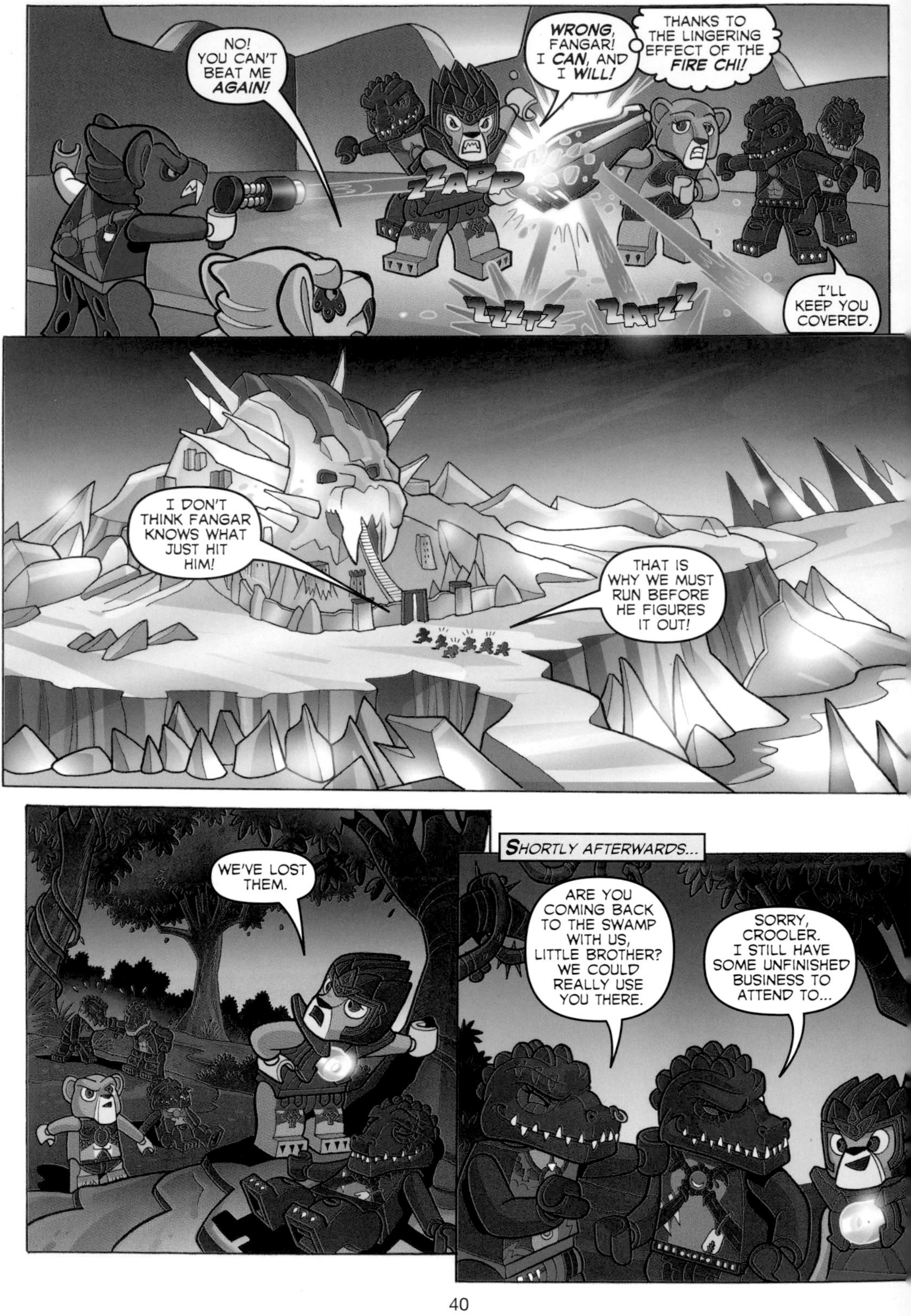
NO! YOU CAN'T BEAT ME AGAIN!
WRONG, FANGAR! I CAN, AND I WILL!
THANKS TO THE LINGERING EFFECT OF THE FIRE CHI!
ZZAPP
ZZZTZ
ZATZZ
I'LL KEEP YOU COVERED.
I DON'T THINK FANGAR KNOWS WHAT JUST HIT HIM!
THAT IS WHY WE MUST RUN BEFORE HE FIGURES IT OUT!
WE'VE LOST THEM.
SHORTLY AFTERWARDS...
ARE YOU COMING BACK TO THE SWAMP WITH US, LITTLE BROTHER? WE COULD REALLY USE YOU THERE.
SORRY, CROOLER. I STILL HAVE SOME UNFINISHED BUSINESS TO ATTEND TO...

ON THE WAY BACK TO THE **PHOENIX TEMPLE,** LAVAL REVEALS A NEW PLAN TO CRAGGER...

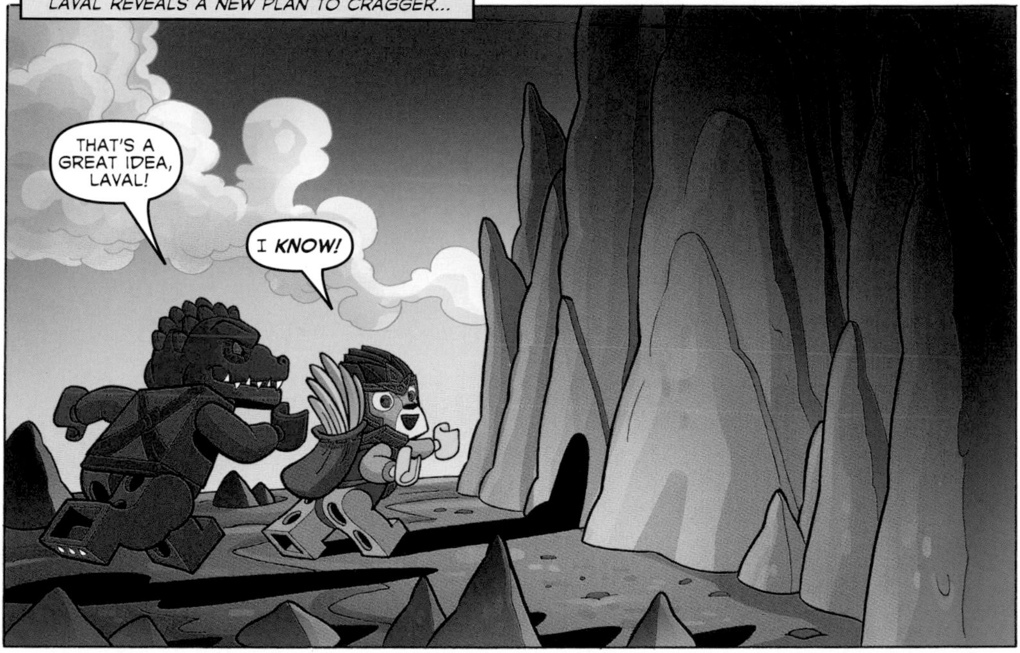
THAT'S A GREAT IDEA, LAVAL!
I ***KNOW!***

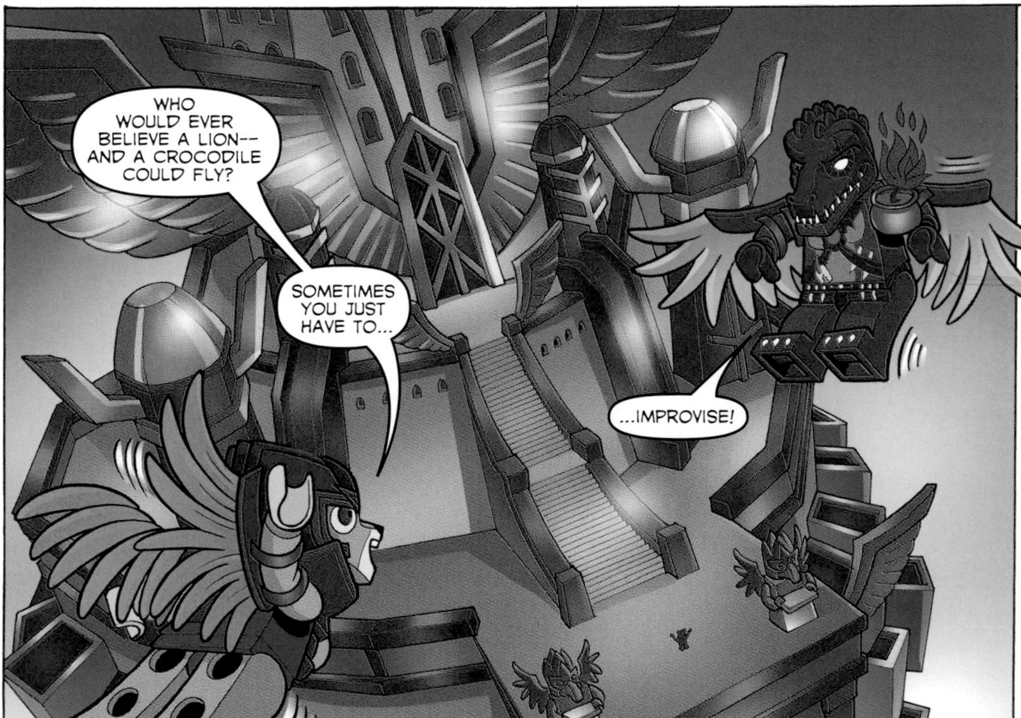
WHO WOULD EVER BELIEVE A LION-- AND A CROCODILE COULD FLY?
SOMETIMES YOU JUST HAVE TO...
...IMPROVISE!
THE END.

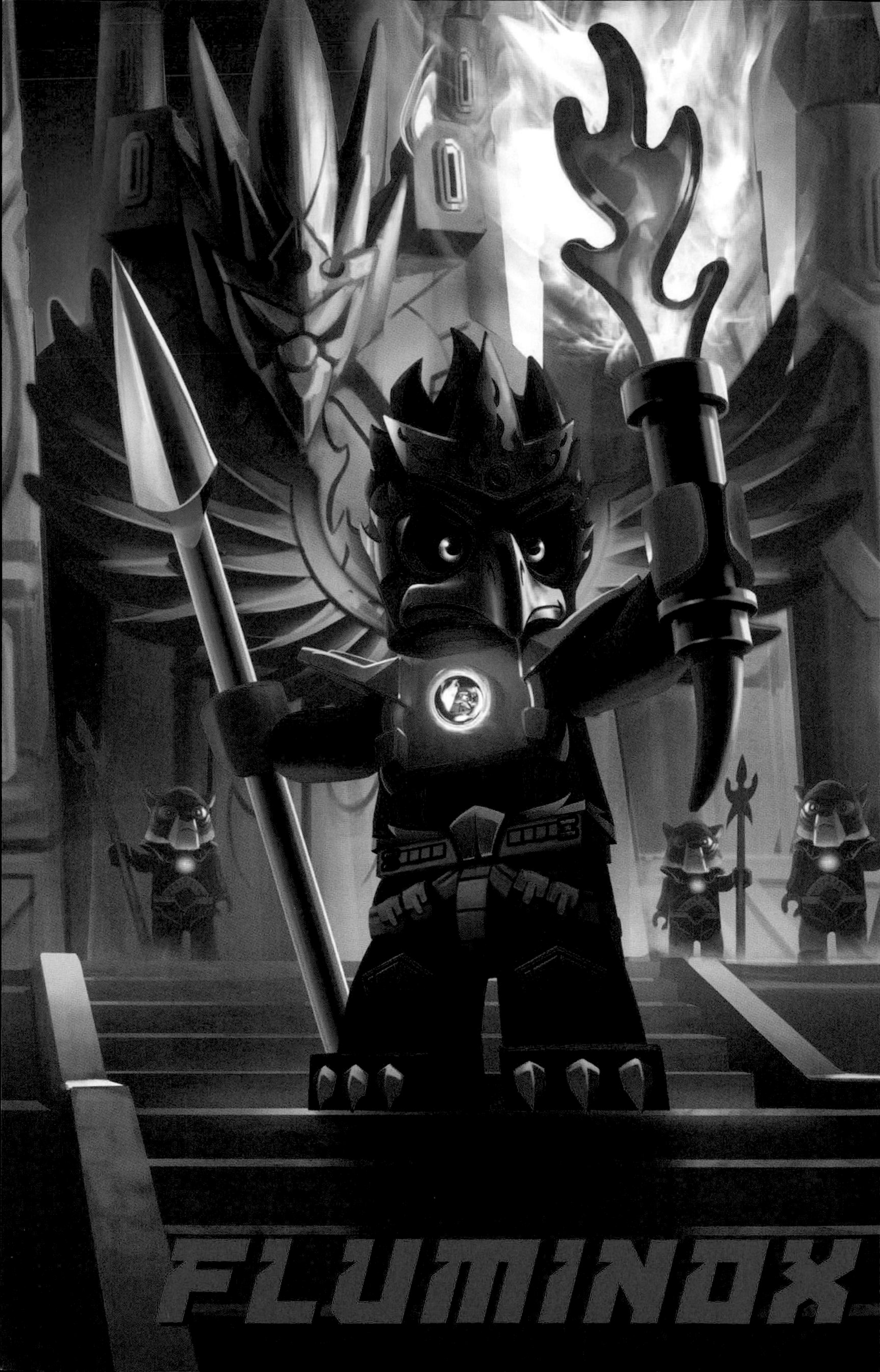
FLUMINOX

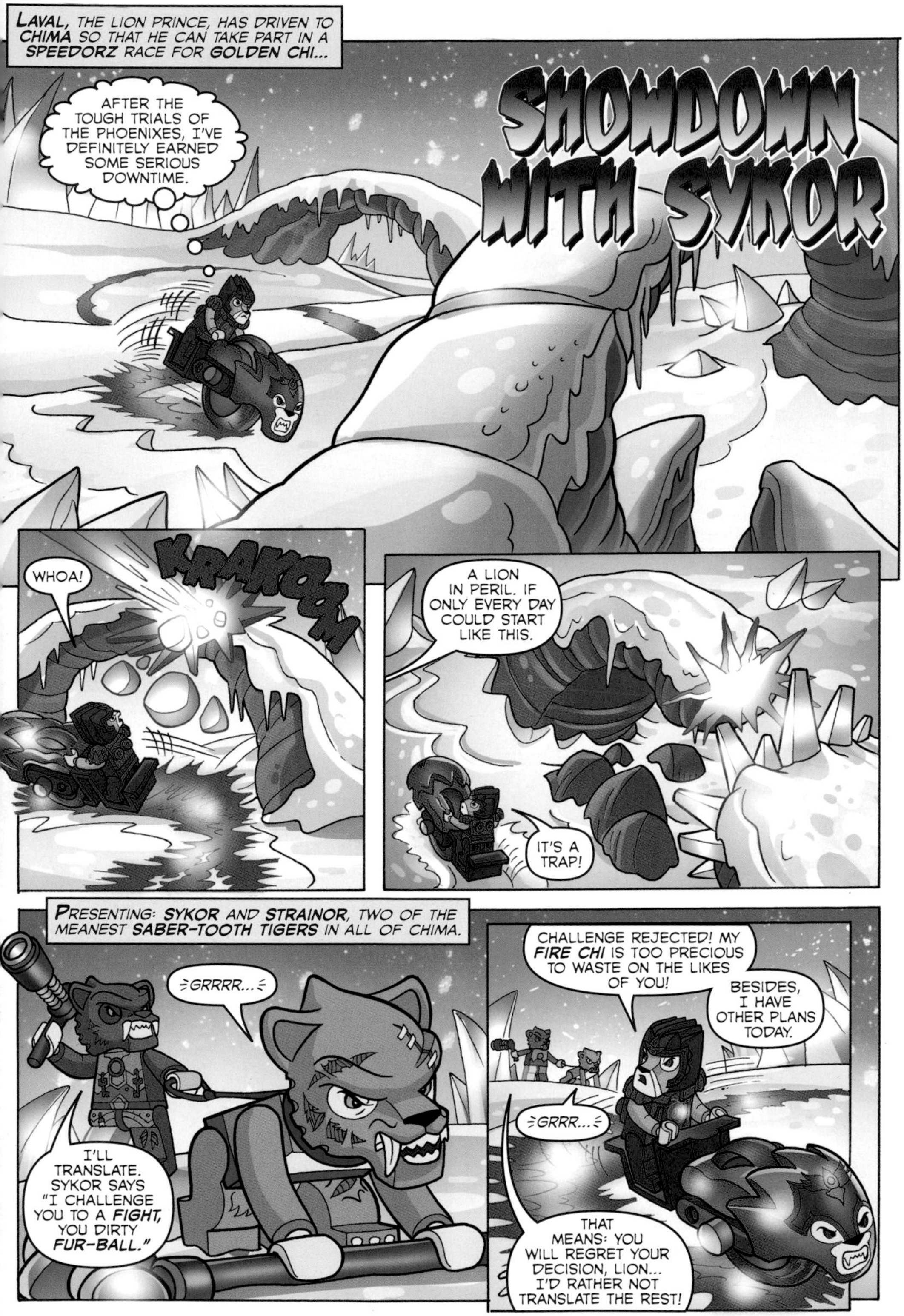
LAVAL, THE LION PRINCE, HAS DRIVEN TO CHIMA SO THAT HE CAN TAKE PART IN A SPEEDORZ RACE FOR GOLDEN CHI...
SHOWDOWN WITH SYKOR
AFTER THE TOUGH TRIALS OF THE PHOENIXES, I'VE DEFINITELY EARNED SOME SERIOUS DOWNTIME.
WHOA!
KRAKOOM
A LION IN PERIL. IF ONLY EVERY DAY COULD START LIKE THIS.
IT'S A TRAP!
PRESENTING: SYKOR AND STRAINOR, TWO OF THE MEANEST SABER-TOOTH TIGERS IN ALL OF CHIMA.
GRRRR...
I'LL TRANSLATE. SYKOR SAYS "I CHALLENGE YOU TO A FIGHT, YOU DIRTY FUR-BALL."
CHALLENGE REJECTED! MY FIRE CHI IS TOO PRECIOUS TO WASTE ON THE LIKES OF YOU!
BESIDES, I HAVE OTHER PLANS TODAY.
GRRR...
THAT MEANS: YOU WILL REGRET YOUR DECISION, LION... I'D RATHER NOT TRANSLATE THE REST!

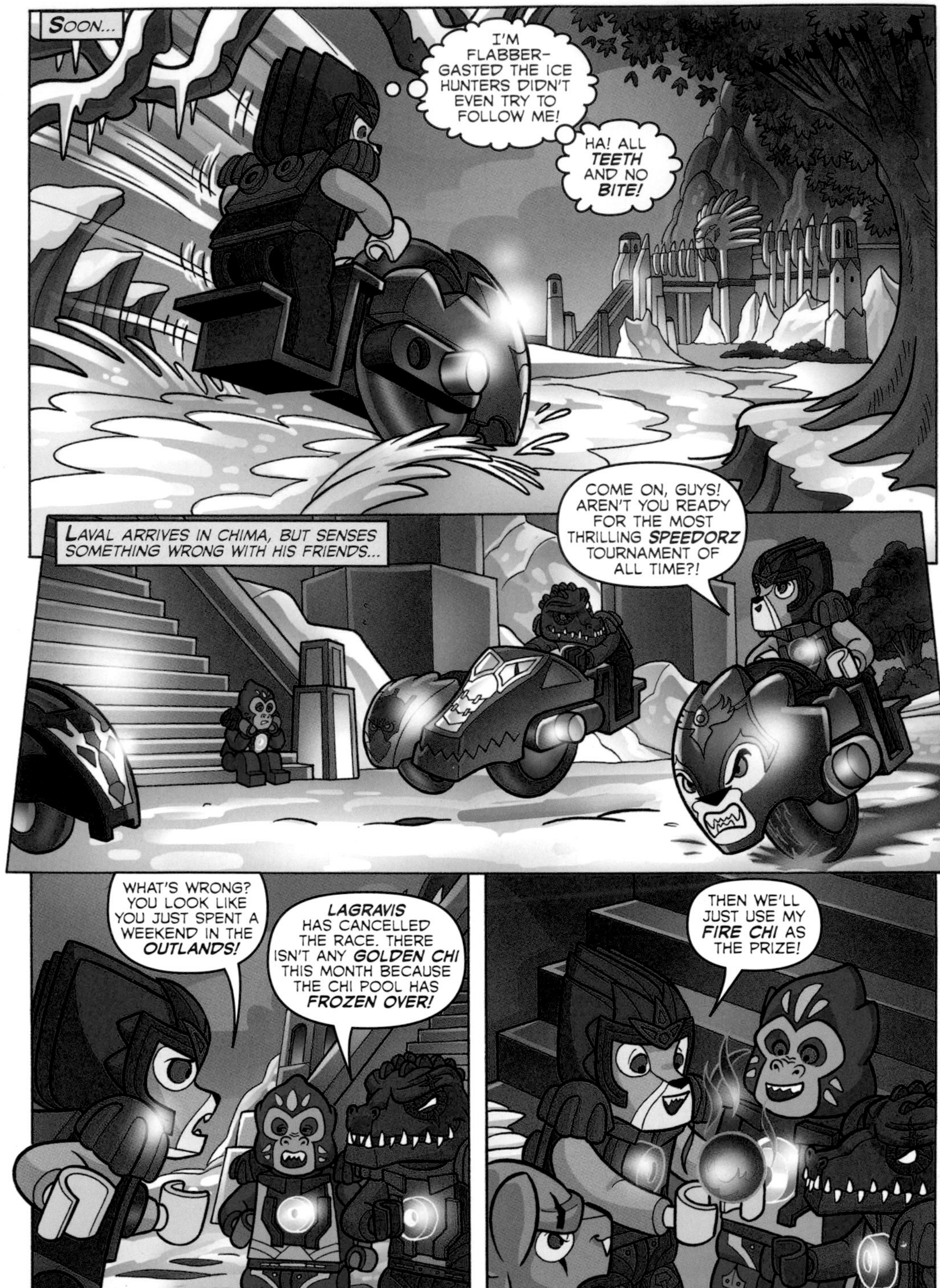
SOON...
I'M FLABBER-GASTED THE ICE HUNTERS DIDN'T EVEN TRY TO FOLLOW ME!
HA! ALL TEETH AND NO BITE!
LAVAL ARRIVES IN CHIMA, BUT SENSES SOMETHING WRONG WITH HIS FRIENDS...
COME ON, GUYS! AREN'T YOU READY FOR THE MOST THRILLING SPEEDORZ TOURNAMENT OF ALL TIME?!
WHAT'S WRONG? YOU LOOK LIKE YOU JUST SPENT A WEEKEND IN THE OUTLANDS!
LAGRAVIS HAS CANCELLED THE RACE. THERE ISN'T ANY GOLDEN CHI THIS MONTH BECAUSE THE CHI POOL HAS FROZEN OVER!
THEN WE'LL JUST USE MY FIRE CHI AS THE PRIZE!

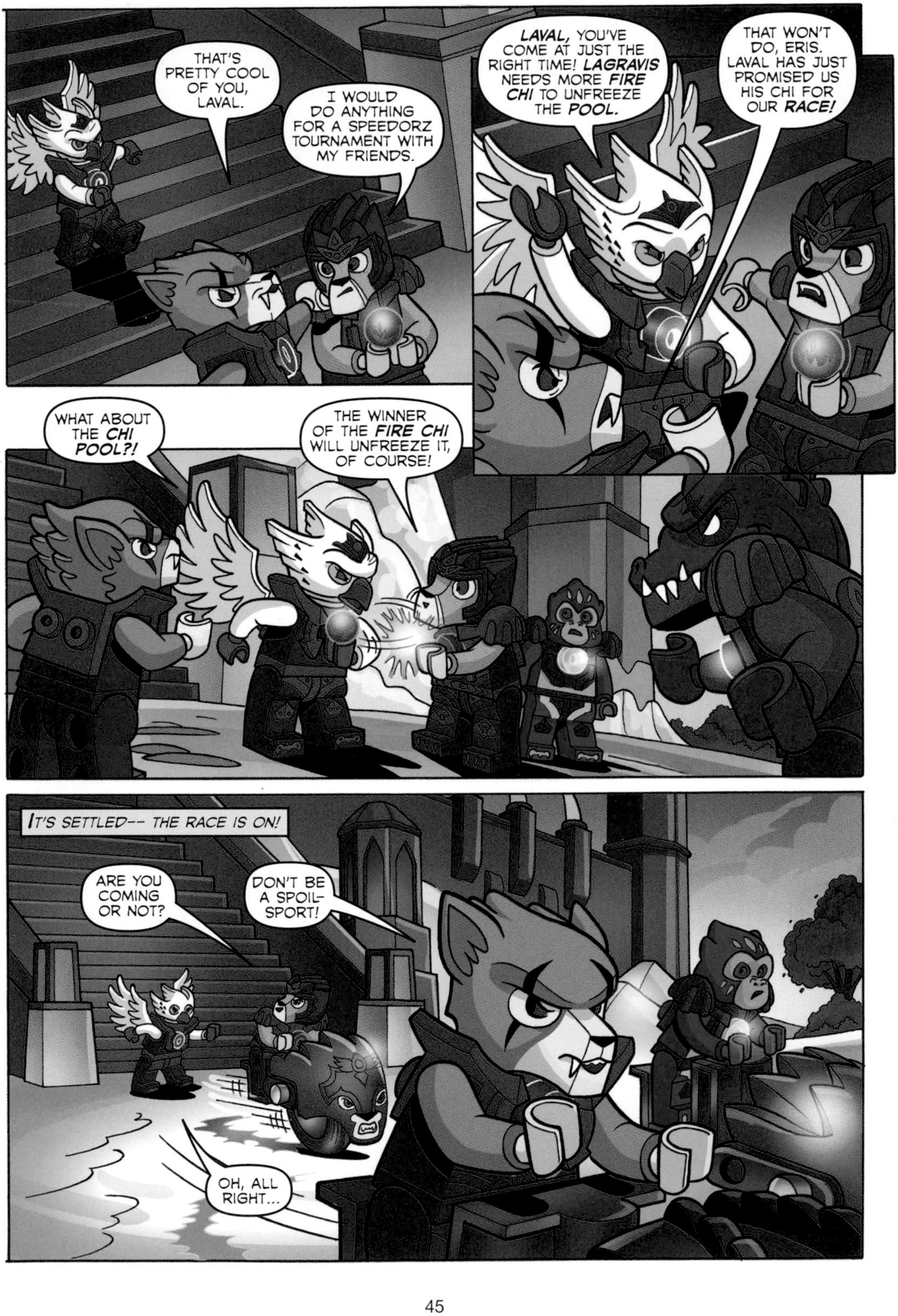
THAT'S PRETTY COOL OF YOU, LAVAL.
I WOULD DO ANYTHING FOR A SPEEDORZ TOURNAMENT WITH MY FRIENDS.
LAVAL, YOU'VE COME AT JUST THE RIGHT TIME! LAGRAVIS NEEDS MORE FIRE CHI TO UNFREEZE THE POOL.
THAT WON'T DO, ERIS. LAVAL HAS JUST PROMISED US HIS CHI FOR OUR RACE!
WHAT ABOUT THE CHI POOL?!
THE WINNER OF THE FIRE CHI WILL UNFREEZE IT, OF COURSE!
IT'S SETTLED-- THE RACE IS ON!
ARE YOU COMING OR NOT?
DON'T BE A SPOIL-SPORT!
OH, ALL RIGHT...

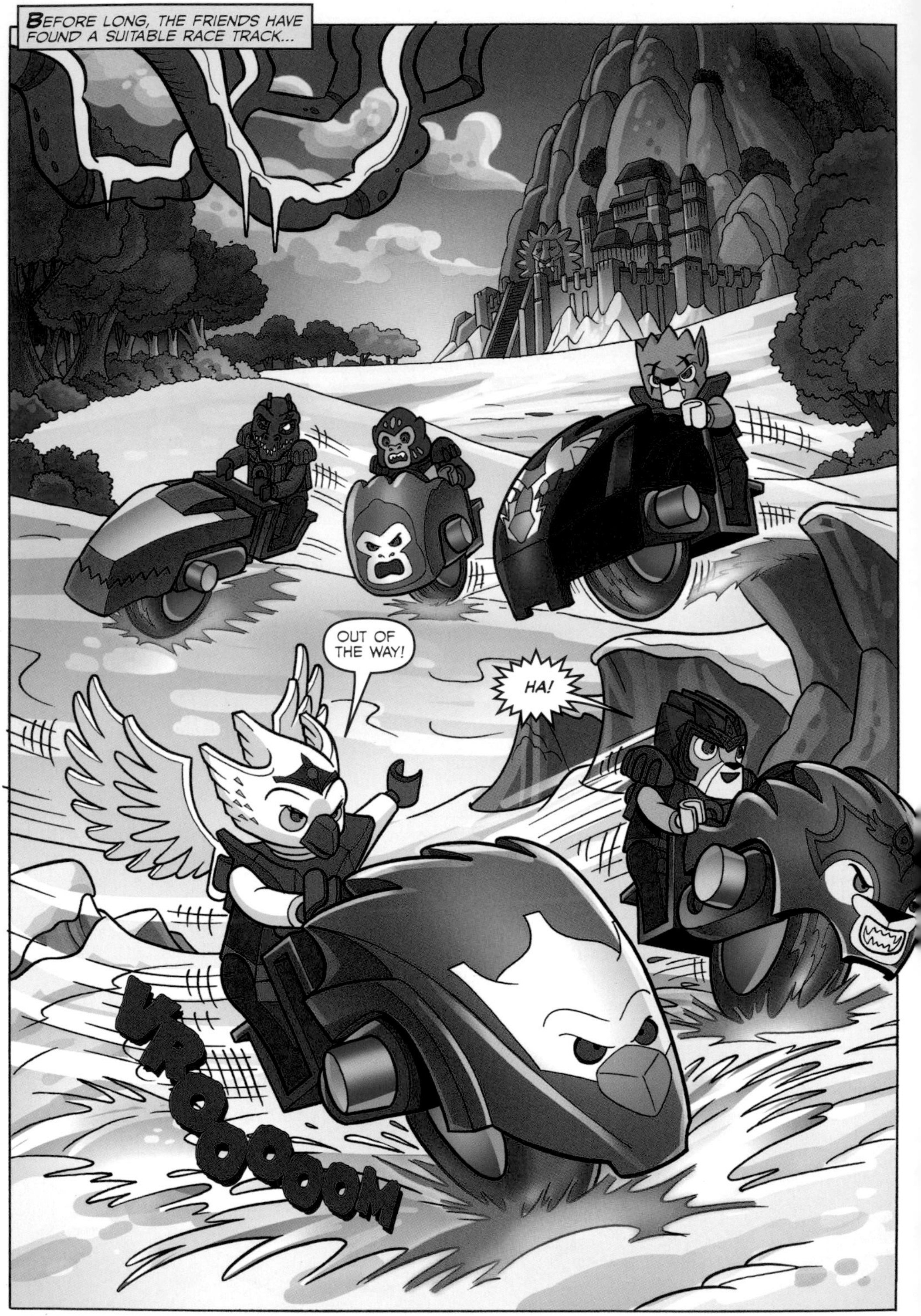
BEFORE LONG, THE FRIENDS HAVE FOUND A SUITABLE RACE TRACK...
OUT OF THE WAY!
HA!
VROOOOOOM

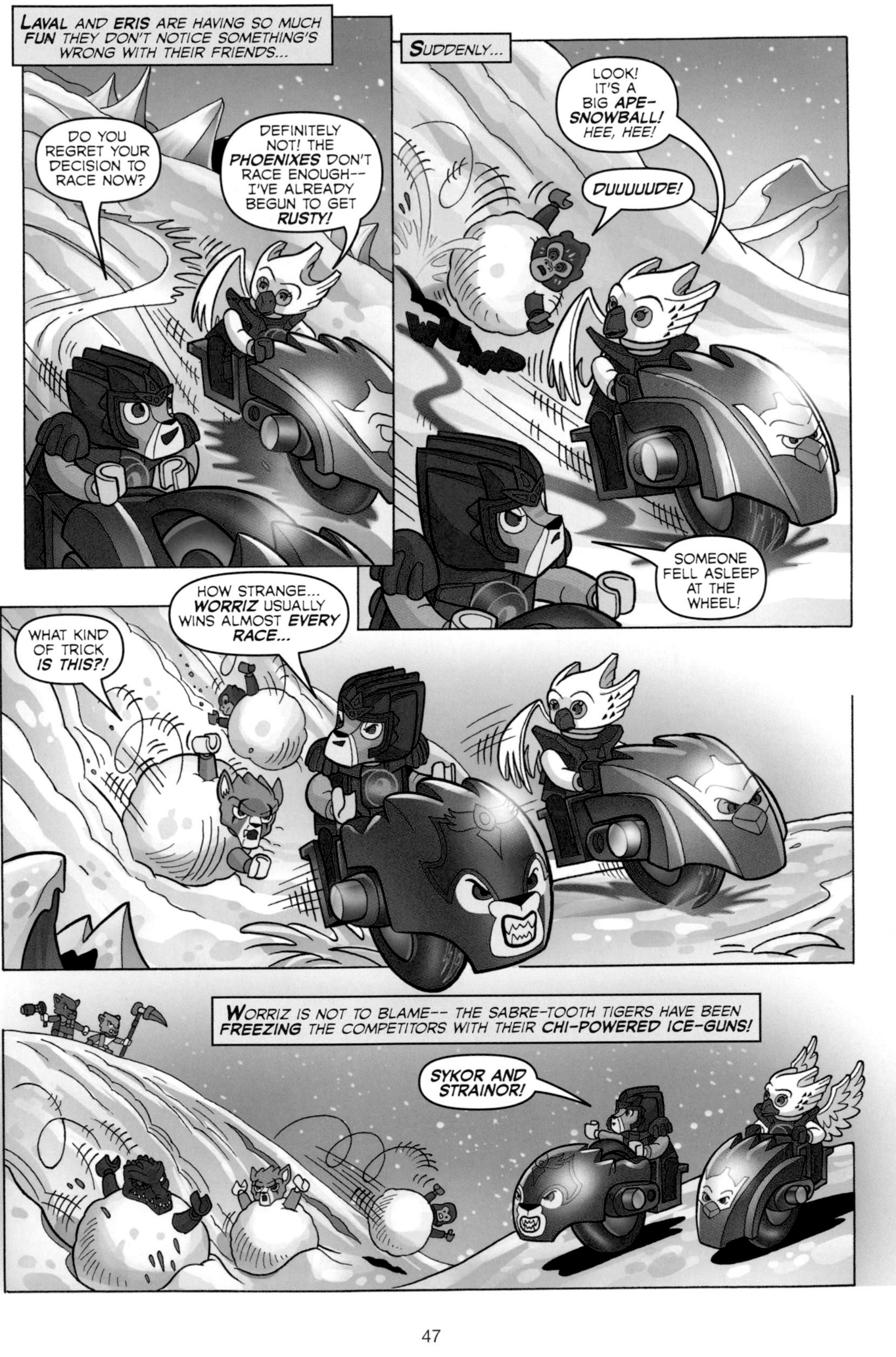
LAVAL AND ERIS ARE HAVING SO MUCH FUN THEY DON'T NOTICE SOMETHING'S WRONG WITH THEIR FRIENDS...
DO YOU REGRET YOUR DECISION TO RACE NOW?
DEFINITELY NOT! THE PHOENIXES DON'T RACE ENOUGH-- I'VE ALREADY BEGUN TO GET RUSTY!
SUDDENLY...
LOOK! IT'S A BIG APE-SNOWBALL! HEE, HEE!
DUUUUUDE!
WUMP
SOMEONE FELL ASLEEP AT THE WHEEL!
WHAT KIND OF TRICK IS THIS?!
HOW STRANGE... WORRIZ USUALLY WINS ALMOST EVERY RACE...
WORRIZ IS NOT TO BLAME-- THE SABRE-TOOTH TIGERS HAVE BEEN FREEZING THE COMPETITORS WITH THEIR CHI-POWERED ICE-GUNS!
SYKOR AND STRAINOR!

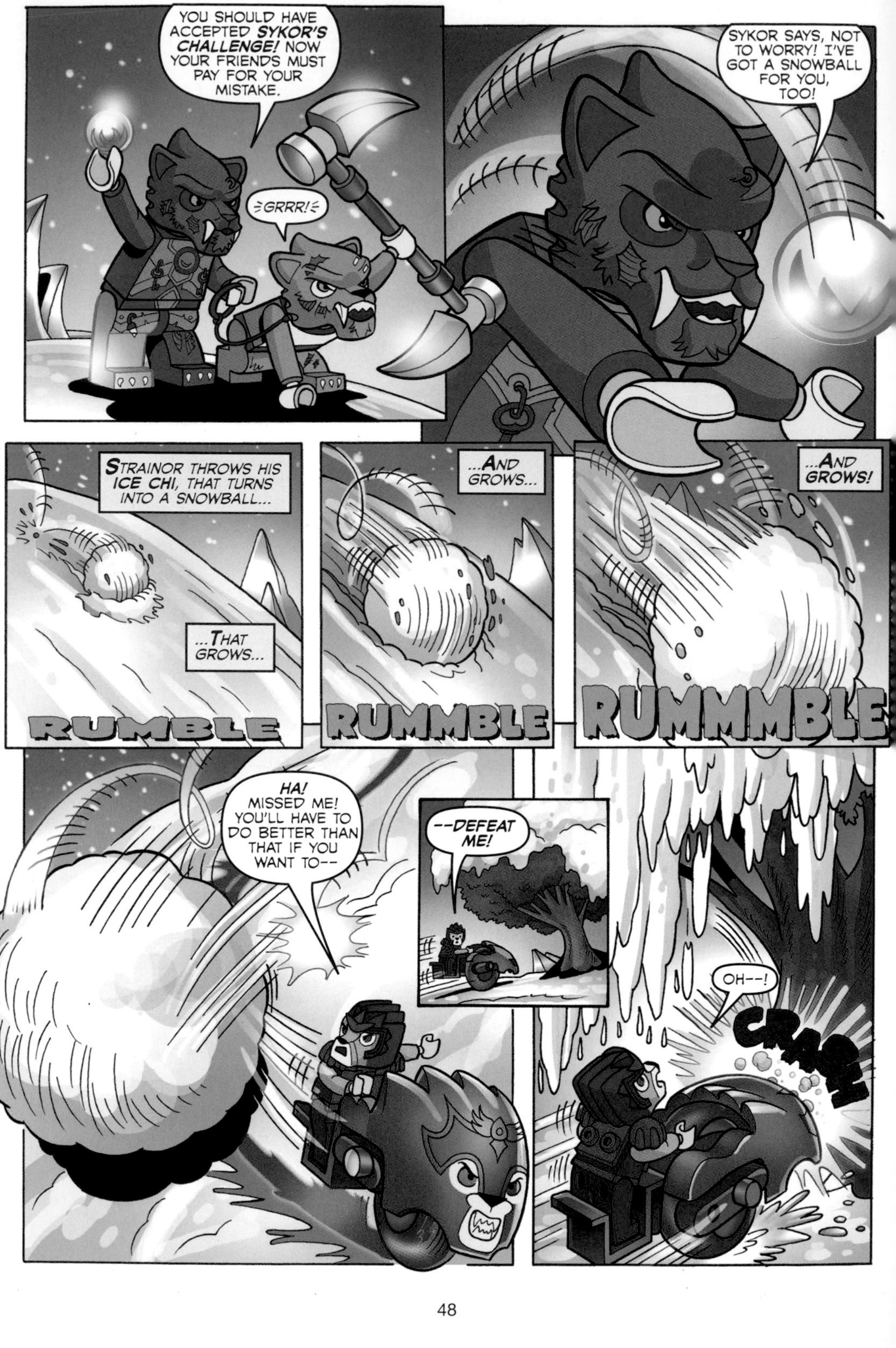
YOU SHOULD HAVE ACCEPTED SYKOR'S CHALLENGE! NOW YOUR FRIENDS MUST PAY FOR YOUR MISTAKE.
GRRR!
SYKOR SAYS, NOT TO WORRY! I'VE GOT A SNOWBALL FOR YOU, TOO!
STRAINOR THROWS HIS ICE CHI, THAT TURNS INTO A SNOWBALL...
...THAT GROWS...
RUMBLE
...AND GROWS...
RUMMBLE
...AND GROWS!
RUMMMBLE
HA! MISSED ME! YOU'LL HAVE TO DO BETTER THAN THAT IF YOU WANT TO--
--DEFEAT ME!
OH--!
CRASH

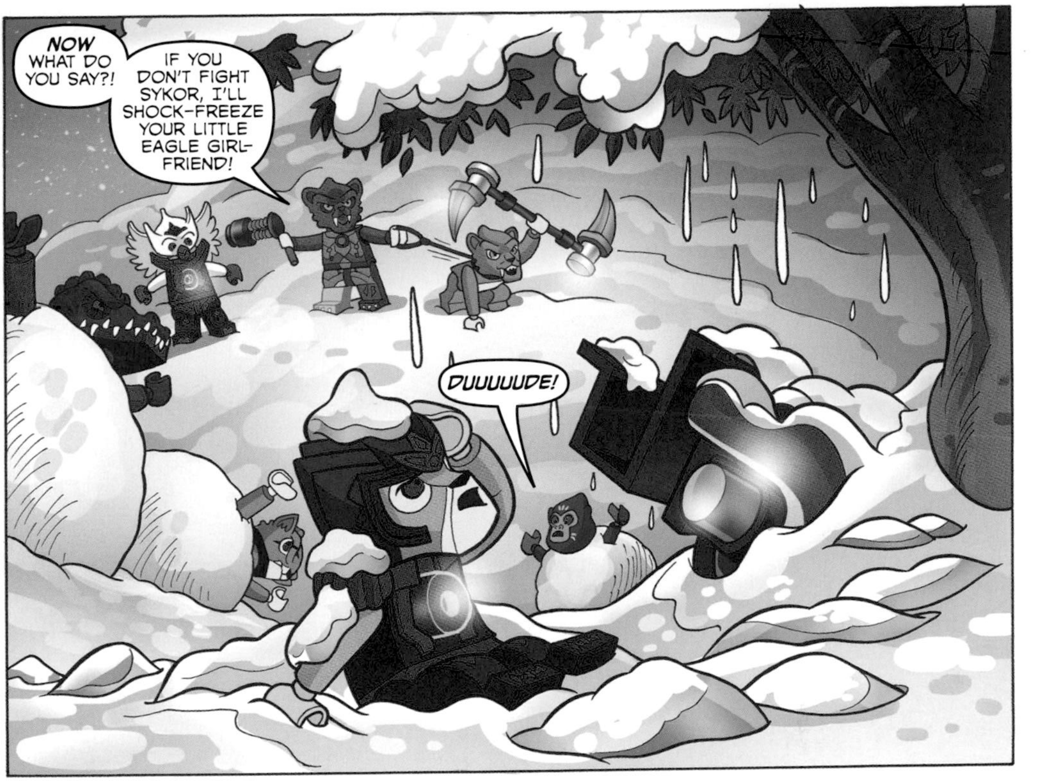
NOW WHAT DO YOU SAY?!
IF YOU DON'T FIGHT SYKOR, I'LL SHOCK-FREEZE YOUR LITTLE EAGLE GIRL-FRIEND!
DUUUUUDE!

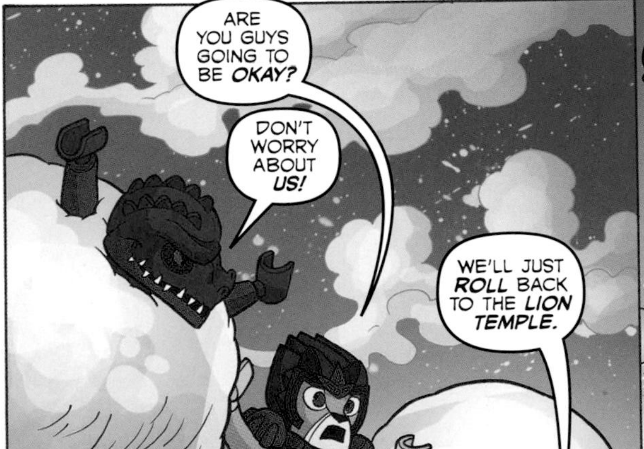
ARE YOU GUYS GOING TO BE OKAY?
DON'T WORRY ABOUT US!
WE'LL JUST ROLL BACK TO THE LION TEMPLE.

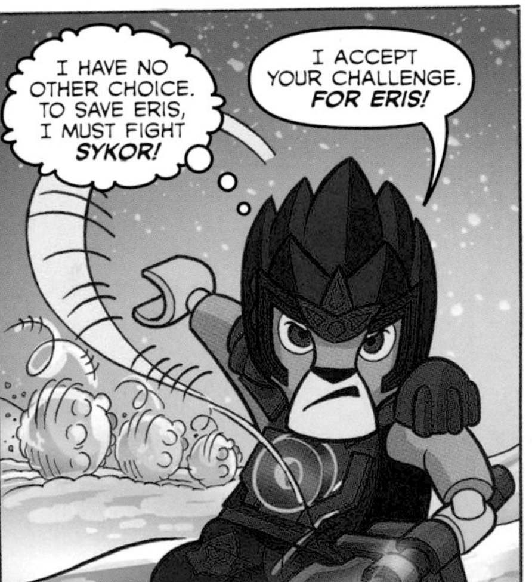
I HAVE NO OTHER CHOICE. TO SAVE ERIS, I MUST FIGHT SYKOR!
I ACCEPT YOUR CHALLENGE. FOR ERIS!

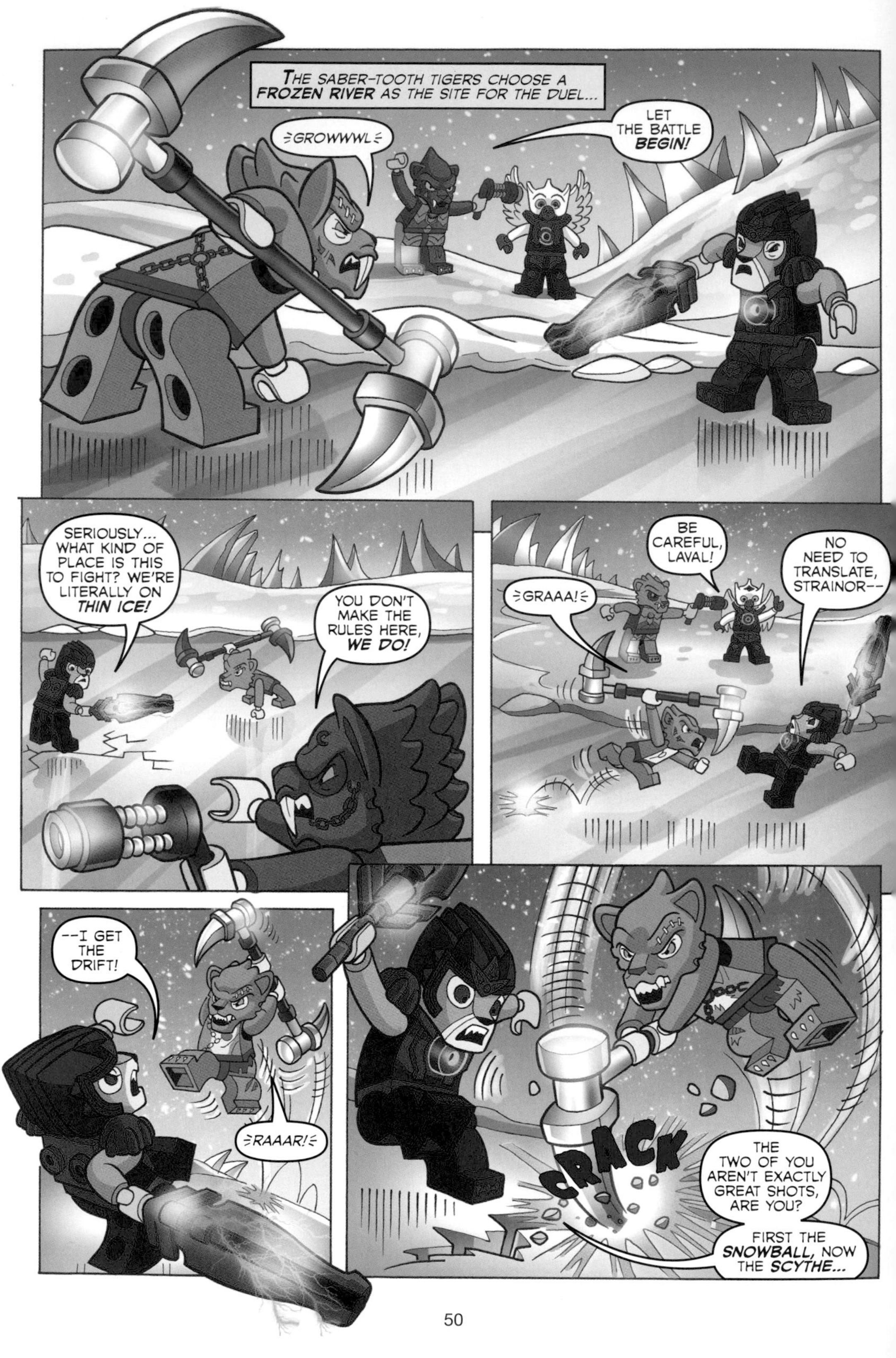
THE SABER-TOOTH TIGERS CHOOSE A FROZEN RIVER AS THE SITE FOR THE DUEL...
GROWWWL
LET THE BATTLE BEGIN!
SERIOUSLY... WHAT KIND OF PLACE IS THIS TO FIGHT? WE'RE LITERALLY ON THIN ICE!
YOU DON'T MAKE THE RULES HERE, WE DO!
BE CAREFUL, LAVAL!
GRAAA!
NO NEED TO TRANSLATE, STRAINOR--
--I GET THE DRIFT!
RAAAR!
CRACK
THE TWO OF YOU AREN'T EXACTLY GREAT SHOTS, ARE YOU?
FIRST THE SNOWBALL, NOW THE SCYTHE...

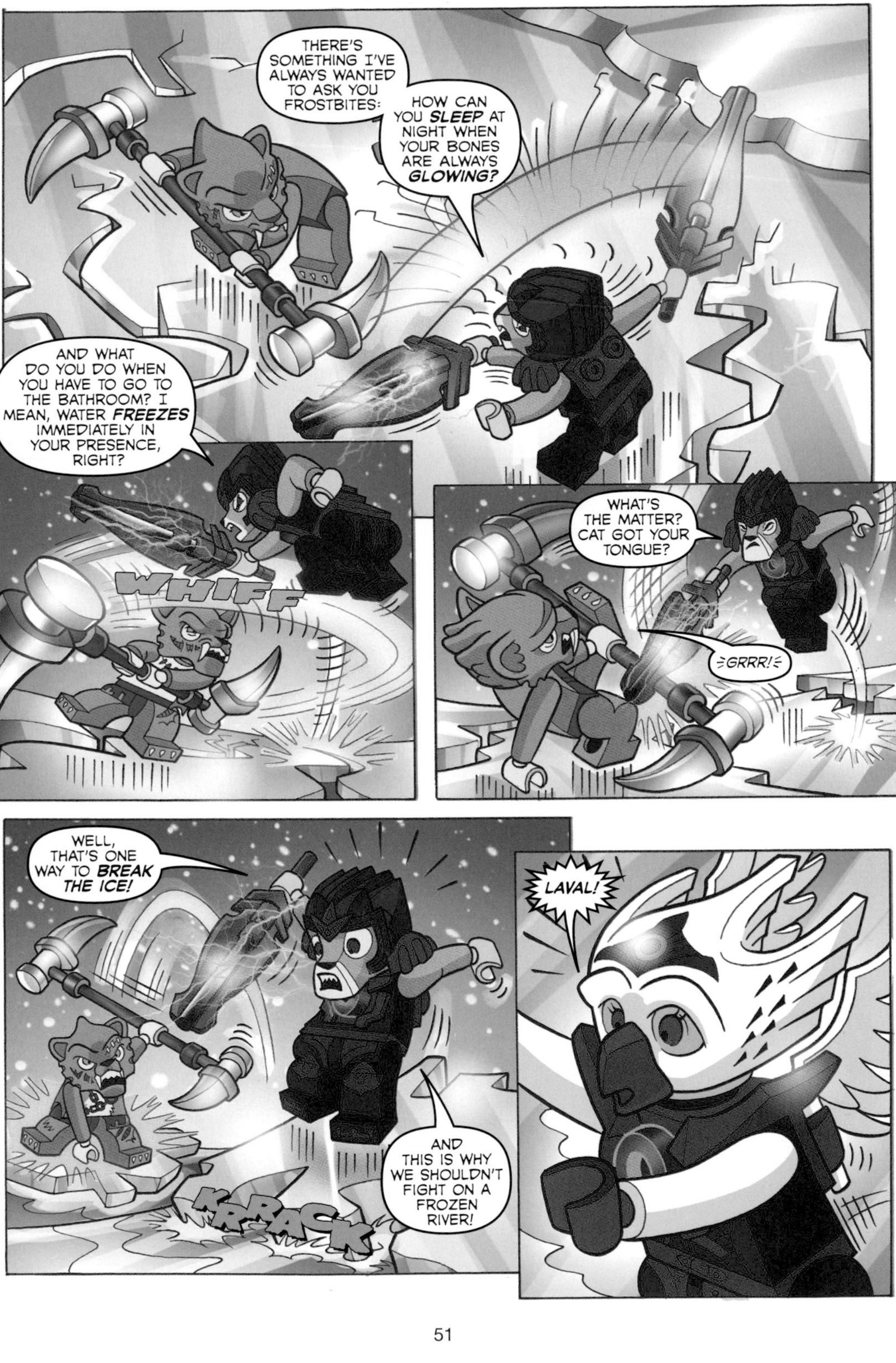
THERE'S SOMETHING I'VE ALWAYS WANTED TO ASK YOU FROSTBITES:
HOW CAN YOU **SLEEP** AT NIGHT WHEN YOUR BONES ARE ALWAYS **GLOWING?**
AND WHAT DO YOU DO WHEN YOU HAVE TO GO TO THE BATHROOM? I MEAN, WATER **FREEZES** IMMEDIATELY IN YOUR PRESENCE, RIGHT?
WHIFF
WHAT'S THE MATTER? CAT GOT YOUR TONGUE?
GRRR!
WELL, THAT'S ONE WAY TO **BREAK THE ICE!**
KRRACK
AND THIS IS WHY WE SHOULDN'T FIGHT ON A FROZEN RIVER!
LAVAL!

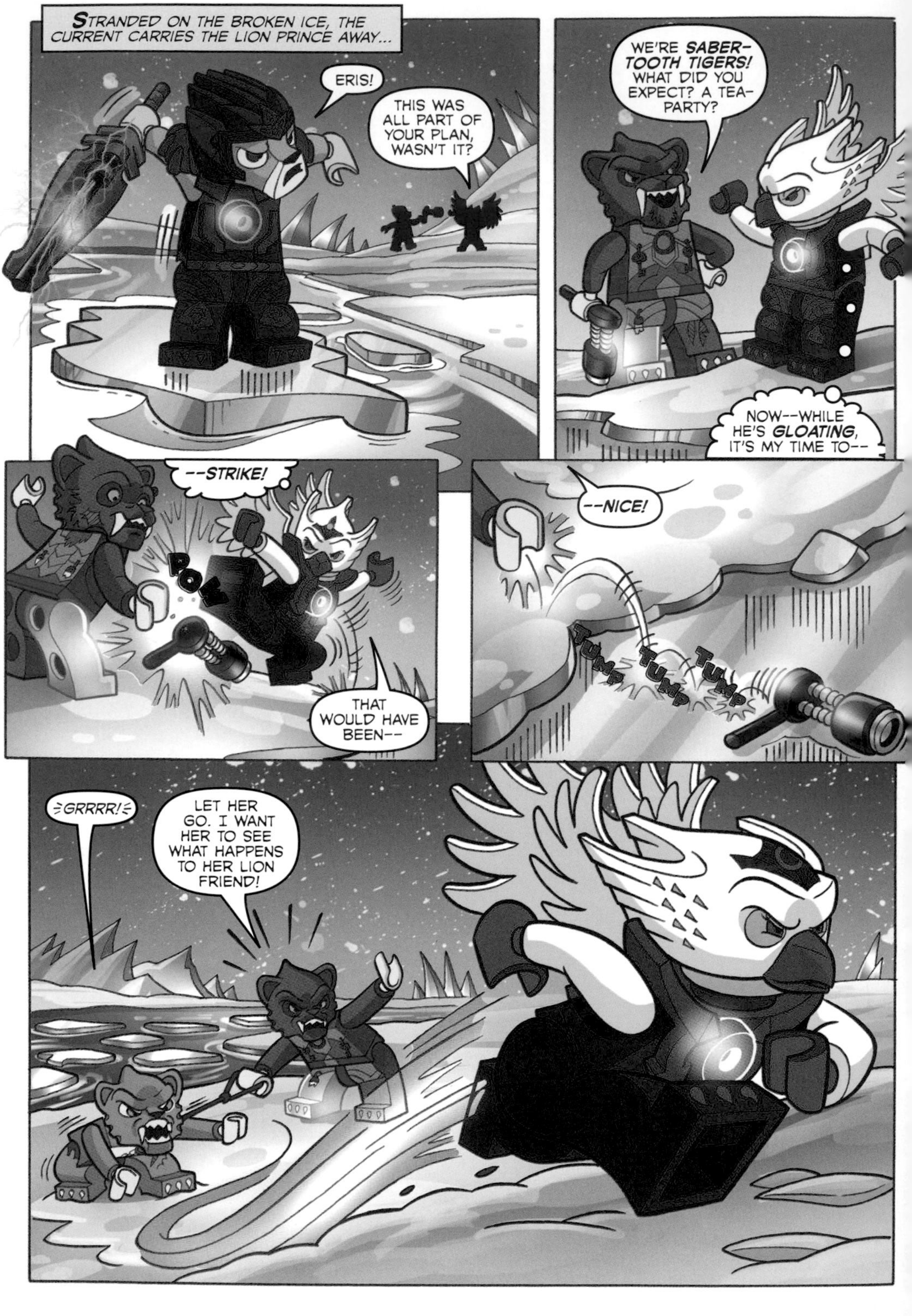
STRANDED ON THE BROKEN ICE, THE CURRENT CARRIES THE LION PRINCE AWAY...
ERIS!
THIS WAS ALL PART OF YOUR PLAN, WASN'T IT?
WE'RE SABER-TOOTH TIGERS! WHAT DID YOU EXPECT? A TEA-PARTY?
NOW--WHILE HE'S GLOATING, IT'S MY TIME TO--
--STRIKE!
POW
THAT WOULD HAVE BEEN--
--NICE!
TUMP TUMP TUMP
GRRRR!
LET HER GO. I WANT HER TO SEE WHAT HAPPENS TO HER LION FRIEND!

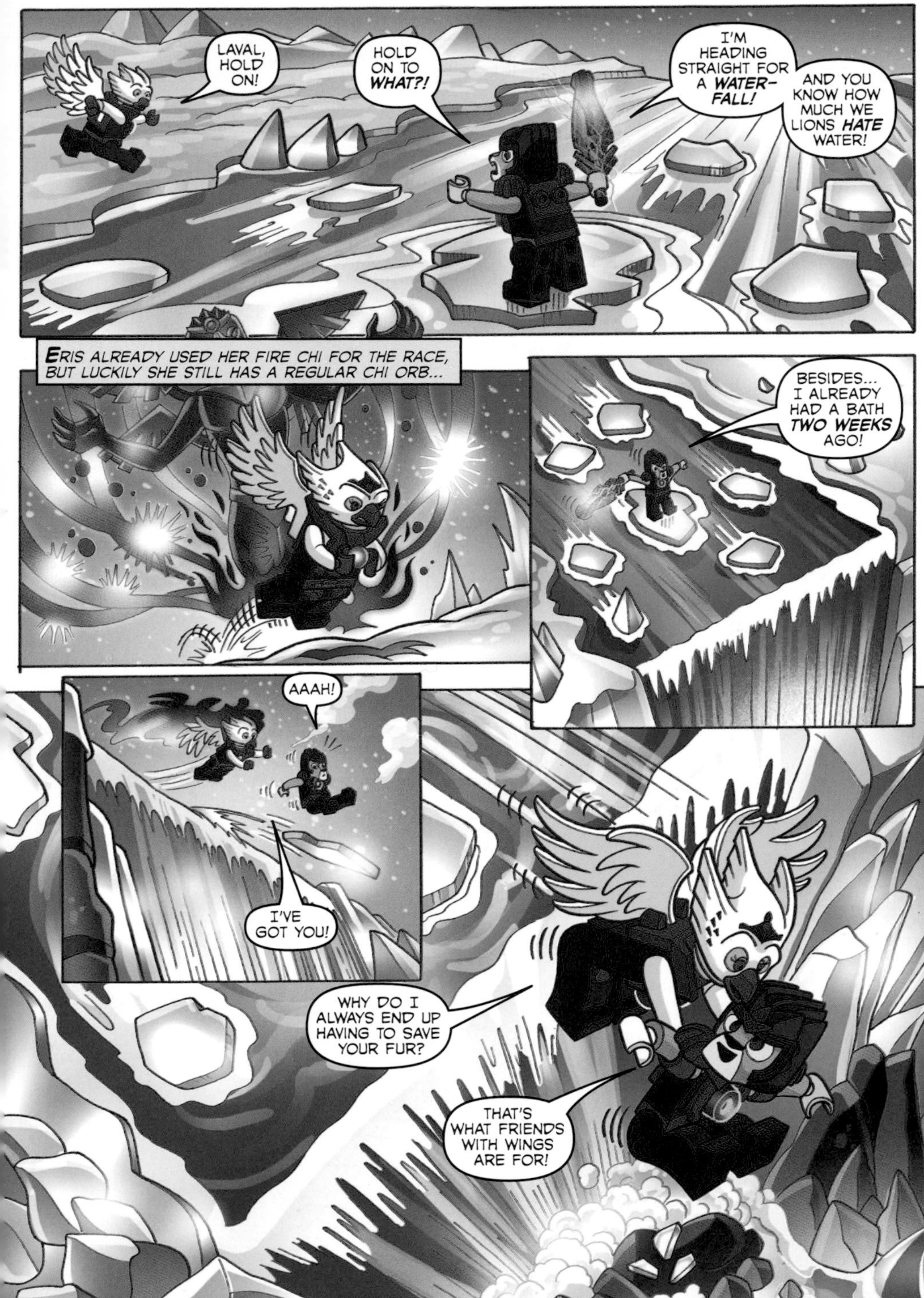
LAVAL, HOLD ON!
HOLD ON TO WHAT?!
I'M HEADING STRAIGHT FOR A WATER-FALL!
AND YOU KNOW HOW MUCH WE LIONS HATE WATER!
ERIS ALREADY USED HER FIRE CHI FOR THE RACE, BUT LUCKILY SHE STILL HAS A REGULAR CHI ORB...
BESIDES... I ALREADY HAD A BATH TWO WEEKS AGO!
AAAH!
I'VE GOT YOU!
WHY DO I ALWAYS END UP HAVING TO SAVE YOUR FUR?
THAT'S WHAT FRIENDS WITH WINGS ARE FOR!

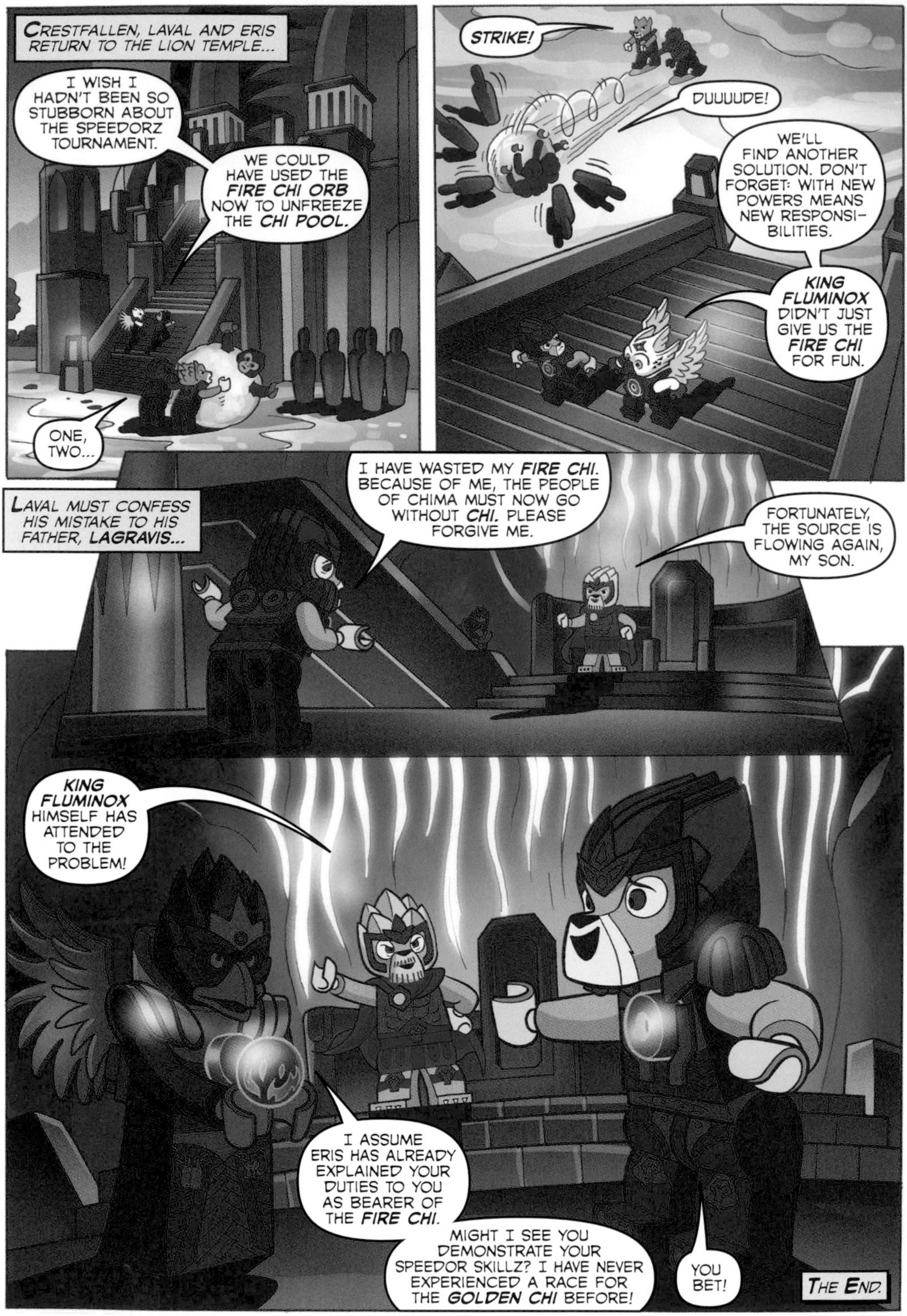
CRESTFALLEN, LAVAL AND ERIS RETURN TO THE LION TEMPLE...
I WISH I HADN'T BEEN SO STUBBORN ABOUT THE SPEEDORZ TOURNAMENT.
WE COULD HAVE USED THE FIRE CHI ORB NOW TO UNFREEZE THE CHI POOL.
ONE, TWO...
STRIKE!
DUUUUDE!
WE'LL FIND ANOTHER SOLUTION. DON'T FORGET: WITH NEW POWERS MEANS NEW RESPONSIBILITIES.
KING FLUMINOX DIDN'T JUST GIVE US THE FIRE CHI FOR FUN.
LAVAL MUST CONFESS HIS MISTAKE TO HIS FATHER, LAGRAVIS...
I HAVE WASTED MY FIRE CHI. BECAUSE OF ME, THE PEOPLE OF CHIMA MUST NOW GO WITHOUT CHI. PLEASE FORGIVE ME.
FORTUNATELY, THE SOURCE IS FLOWING AGAIN, MY SON.
KING FLUMINOX HIMSELF HAS ATTENDED TO THE PROBLEM!
I ASSUME ERIS HAS ALREADY EXPLAINED YOUR DUTIES TO YOU AS BEARER OF THE FIRE CHI.
MIGHT I SEE YOU DEMONSTRATE YOUR SPEEDOR SKILLZ? I HAVE NEVER EXPERIENCED A RACE FOR THE GOLDEN CHI BEFORE!
YOU BET!
THE END.

WATCH OUT FOR PAPERCUTZ™

Welcome to the thrilling, totally-tantalizing third LEGO® LEGENDS OF CHIMA graphic novel, by Yannick Grotholt and Comicon, from Papercutz—those humble humanoids dedicated to publishing great graphic novels for all ages. I'm Jim Salicrup, the Earth-bound Editor-in-Chief—not to be confused with the Editor-with-CHI! We've got a lot to talk about, so let's get right to it!

When we're not working away on creating great graphic novels at our palatial Papercutz offices, chances are we're probably at a comicbook convention somewhere, trying to get the word out about such graphic novels as LEGO LEGENDS OF CHIMA, LEGO NINJAGO, ANNOYING ORANGE, and many others. Probably the biggest convention every year has to be Comic-Con International: San Diego, better known as the San Diego Comic-Con. Papercutz has been exhibiting at this colossal comic-con since we published our very first graphic novels back in 2005, and it's always fun to meet both current and future Papercutz fans. Of course, we're eager to attract as many LEGO fans as possible too, after all LEGO exhibits at Comic-Con as well. Usually all it takes is displaying the latest LEGO LEGENDS OF CHIMA and LEGO NINJAGO graphic novels at our booth, and LEGO fans immediately take notice. We also run episodes from the animated LEGO LEGENDS OF CHIMA and LEGO NINJAGO TV series, and have often had fans stand in front of our TV monitor completely transfixed—sometimes even mouthing every line of dialogue along with the show! This is even more incredible than it sounds because you wouldn't believe how much other media is vying for fans' attention at these cons.

But every now and then we're surprised when an unexpected guest drops by our booth, and this year we were honored to have none other than the LEGO Group's own Tommy Andreasen stop by. Tommy had flown in to San Diego especially to appear on several of the LEGO Group's panels, telling fans exactly what to expect from the LEGO Group in 2014, 2015, and beyond. Somehow, Tommy was able to wend his way through the crowded Comic-Con corridors and make his way through to our booth! He's one of the big creative guys at the LEGO Group, involved with "Concepts & Stories," and had a big role in developing LEGO LEGENDS OF CHIMA, so we were truly honored that he came by to see us!

From Left to Right: a Rabbid, John Cena, Jim Salicrup, Tommy Andreasen, and Michael Petranek. [Photo by Cherie Tieri.]

Tommy checks out the LEGO LEGENDS OF CHIMA graphic novel. [Photo by Cherie Tieri.]

To be perfectly clear, we're excited to meet everyone who visits us at conventions. It's so great to actually meet the people we're creating these graphic novels for, and to hear their feedback. We can easily get swept up by all the work that's involved in putting these books together, that's it's great to be reminded that there are people out there as excited as we are about them.

Speaking of which, we better get back to work! Now we have to start putting LEGO LEGENDS OF CHIMA #4 together! Think there's a CHI for that?

Thanks,

Jim

STAY IN TOUCH!

EMAIL:	salicrup@papercutz.com
WEB:	papercutz.com
TWITTER:	@papercutzgn
FACEBOOK:	PAPERCUTZGRAPHICNOVELS
FAN MAIL:	Papercutz, 160 Broadway, Suite 700, East Wing, New York, NY 10038

LEGO® GRAPHIC NOVELS AVAILABLE FROM PAPERCUTZ™

LEGO NINJAGO #1

LEGO NINJAGO #2

LEGO NINJAGO #3

LEGO NINJAGO #4

LEGO NINJAGO #5

LEGO NINJAGO #6

LEGO NINJAGO #7

LEGO NINJAGO #8

SPECIAL EDITION #1
(Features stories from LEGO
NINJAGO #1 & #2.)

SPECIAL EDITION #2
(Features stories from LEGO
NINJAGO #3 & #4.)

SPECIAL EDITION #3
(Features stories from LEGO
NINJAGO #5 & #6.)

LEGO NINJAGO #9

**LEGO® NINJAGO graphic novels are available in paper-
back and hardcover at booksellers everywhere.**

LEGO® NINJAGO #1-11 are $6.99 in paperback, and $10.99 in
hardcover. LEGO NINJAGO SPECIAL EDITION #1-3 are $10.99 in
paperback only. You can also order online at papercutz.com. Or call
1-800-886-1223, Monday through Friday, 9 – 5 EST. MC, Visa, and
AmEx accepted. To order by mail, please add $4.00 for postage
and handling for first book ordered, $1.00 for each additional book
and make check payable to NBM Publishing. Send to: Papercutz,
160 Broadway, Suite 700, East Wing, New York, NY 10038.

LEGO NINJAGO graphic novels are also available digitally
wherever e-books are sold.

LEGO NINJAGO #10

LEGO NINJAGO #11